"I wanted to wish yo[...] Christmas."

Joe had waited for her. He'd lit tall red tapers set in tin cans, had carols playing on the jukebox. He handed her a glass. "A toast," he whispered huskily. "To us." The gleam in his eye sent ripples of pleasure through her. "There *is* an us, right, Sara?"

She could no longer evade what had almost happened between them in the storeroom and in the snowed-in cabin. "Yes, Joe, I think we can be friends."

"And what about being more than friends?" He placed a finger under her chin and forced her to look at him. "You know, I never expected when I came back here that I'd want to spend every minute of my time with you."

"Then you're not angry at me for kidnapping you and keeping you in Christmas?" She almost dared not ask.

Joe smiled. "Your heart was in the right place." He took the glass from her hands and pulled her into his arms. "Now, about us being friends..." His mouth lowered, till he was but a whisper away. "Why don't we let this kiss decide...."

Dear Reader,

As the hectic holiday season begins, take a moment to treat yourself to a fantastic love story from Harlequin American Romance. All four of our wonderful books this month are sure to please your every reading fancy.

Beloved author Cathy Gillen Thacker presents us with *A Cowboy Kind of Daddy,* the fourth and final title in her series THE McCABES OF TEXAS. Travis McCabe is the last eligible bachelor in the family and you know his matchmaking parents are not about to let him miss heading to the altar.

Also wrapping up this month is our special series DELIVERY ROOM DADS. Judy Christenberry's memorable *Baby 2000* has a truly heroic McIntyre brother caring for an expectant mother who just may have the first baby of the millennium.

Two holiday stories finish up the month with tales that will bring you lots of seasonal joy. Pamela Bauer pens a delightful small-town romance with *Saving Christmas,* and Jacqueline Diamond brings us an emotional story of unexpected reunions with *Mistletoe Daddy.*

Here's hoping your holiday season is filled with happiness, good health—and lots of romance!

Melissa Jeglinski
Associate Senior Editor

Saving Christmas

PAMELA BAUER

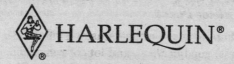

HARLEQUIN®

TORONTO • NEW YORK • LONDON
AMSTERDAM • PARIS • SYDNEY • HAMBURG
STOCKHOLM • ATHENS • TOKYO • MILAN • MADRID
PRAGUE • WARSAW • BUDAPEST • AUCKLAND

ISBN 0-373-16803-9

SAVING CHRISTMAS

Copyright © 1999 by Pamela Muelhbauer.

ABOUT THE AUTHOR

Pamela Bauer is an award-winning author, who was born and raised in Minnesota and still makes her home in a small town not far from Minneapolis. She created Christmas, Minnesota, and all of the characters in it, but visit any one of the small towns that dot the landscape in the upper Midwest and you'll find the people have the same sense of community and generosity of spirit as the residents of her fictional town. That's why Pamela often uses the Midwest as a setting for her novels. It's a great place to fall in love. She ought to know. It's where she met her real-life hero, her husband, Gerr. They've been married twenty-eight years and still find Minnesota one of the most romantic places to be.

Books by Pamela Bauer

HARLEQUIN AMERICAN ROMANCE
668—THE PICK-UP MAN
718—MAIL ORDER COWBOY
803—SAVING CHRISTMAS

And watch for CORPORATE COWBOY, available in February 2000.

Prologue

Nine-year-old Nikki Gibson raced out of the house chanting, "'Star light, star bright, first star I see tonight, wish I may, wish I might, have my wish come true tonight.'" She came to a stop in front of the wooden lawn swing, squeezed her eyes shut and made her wish.

When she opened her eyes, her two cousins, Shawna and Lindsey, were at her side. They were seven and five, which explained why they followed her around wherever she went. Nikki didn't mind. They were the next-best thing to having sisters.

As the three girls sat down on the lawn swing, Nikki took the middle, sliding an arm around each of her cousins protectively. They gently swung back and forth, tipping their heads back to gaze up at the stars.

"What did you wish for, Nikki?" Lindsey, the younger of the two, wanted to know.

"She can't tell or it won't come true," Shawna scolded her for even asking.

Nikki knew that Shawna was right. Not once had she told a single person what it was she wished for when she saw the first star in the sky. Not even her best friend, Chelsea.

She couldn't. Because she wasn't simply wishing on

a star. Nikki knew that on the other side of the stars was heaven, and each of the millions and billions of stars in the sky was a tiny window giving off heaven's light. Every time she looked up at the sky and saw a star, she made sure she didn't miss the chance to say hello to her mother.

"You guys are lucky you live in the hills," Nikki said on a sigh. "You get to see the stars at night."

"Don't you like living on the beach?" Shawna asked.

"Yeah, but I wish it wasn't so overcast. Lots of times I can't see the stars at night." Which bothered Nikki a lot. She needed that peek into heaven every night.

"Are you going to come stay with us for Christmas vacation?" Lindsey sat forward, her eyes widening at the thought.

Before Nikki could answer, Shawna said, "Mama already told you she can't. She has to go to Minnesota."

"Not for the whole vacation," Nikki inserted.

"But I thought your grandma had a broken foot."

"She does, but Dad says that he'll figure out a way to get her to come back here. We're only going to go get her because she's being stubborn," Nikki explained. "Dad says most of the people in the town of Christmas are stubborn."

Shawna giggled. "I never heard of a town called Christmas."

"That's because it's so small. My dad says there's nothing to do there but watch the grass grow in the summer and complain about how cold it is in the winter."

"Is that where Santa Claus lives?" Lindsey wanted to know.

Nikki smiled to herself. She knew that the Santa her

five-year-old cousin referred to was really her uncle Charlie, who dressed up in the red suit and paid a visit to their house on Christmas Eve. Although Shawna was old enough to question Santa's existence, Lindsey still believed in the mythical character and Nikki would never tell her he really didn't exist.

"No, Santa lives at the North Pole," she explained. "Christmas is just an itty-bitty town stuck in the middle of nowhere. My grandma says sometimes it looks like the North Pole because they get so much snow."

"But how can you ride your bike if there's snow?" Lindsey asked.

Again it was Shawna who answered, as if she were an authority on Minnesota winters. "You have to take a sleigh ride."

"Or you can ski," Nikki added.

"Do they have stars?" Lindsey wanted to know.

"My grandma said they do," Nikki replied, hoping that she was right. It was going to be hard enough leaving her cousins to go to Minnesota. If there were no stars there, it would be twice as hard.

"Nikki! We're leaving," her father's voice called from somewhere in the vicinity of the house.

She reluctantly slid off the swing. "I gotta go." She gave each of her cousins a hug, saying, "Be good, okay? And don't worry. This is going to be a great Christmas. And remember, wishes do come true."

As she ran toward the car, she called back to them, "Don't forget to wish upon a star."

Chapter One

December 1, 8:00 p.m.

"I nominate Sara Richards," came a voice from the group assembled in the town hall.

"I second," came several others in unison.

Sara popped up out of her chair. "I'm sorry, but I can't accept the nomination."

No one paid any attention. It was as if she were invisible. They all looked right through her.

Mayor Ed Callahan wasted no time with the vote. "All in favor, say aye."

A collective "Aye" resounded in the crowded hall.

"All opposed?"

"Nay!" It was only one voice. Sara's.

With the thud of a gavel the mayor announced, "Consider it passed that Sara Richards is now the chair of the committee to save Christmas. Sara, you have thirty days to save the town."

Then he thumped his gavel again, saying, "This meeting is adjourned."

Everyone ignored Sara, who stood flapping her arms in protest. The residents picked up their coats, folded their folding chairs and carried them to the rack at the back of the room before heading for the exit. Many of them smiled and waved at her, throwing such compliments her way as "You'll do a good job" and "Glad you're home." And not one of them looked the least bit guilty at having railroaded her into a job she didn't want.

Sara rushed to the table at the head of the room where the mayor and the three-city council representatives sat. "I didn't accept the nomination," she protested. "If this is parliamentary procedure, you're supposed to ask me if I accept the nomination."

"But, Sara, you were the one who said we needed a committee to get organized," Ed Callahan pointed out while the others bobbed their heads in agreement.

"But I didn't say I wanted to *be* the committee."

"Then why did you come to the meeting?"

Well, she certainly wouldn't have come had she known that by simply being in the room and making a suggestion she would be put in charge. She had only been in town two days and already she had been roped into heading a committee—and not just any committee, but the one that was supposed to work a miracle and save the town of Christmas.

"Mom? Dad?" She appealed to her parents, who, she guessed, would have made just as hasty a retreat as the rest of the town's citizens had Sara not stopped them.

"You'll do a fine job, dear," Eugenia Richards said. "Remember when you were senior class president and the school board threatened to do away with school dances because they were having financial difficulties? You single-handedly organized a committee to save the prom."

"That was ten years ago, and saving a high-school dance is not exactly the same thing as saving a town!"

Her mother patted her hand. "You'll be just fine."

"But I don't want to be just fine," Sara spit out irritably, then, realizing it didn't matter what she wanted, sank down onto the chair vacated by the mayor. "I didn't come home because I wanted to do my civic duty."

Her father finally spoke. "Even though you haven't lived here for a while, this town is just as much yours as it is anybody else's. Your roots are here, Sara. Your heritage is here. Do you really want to lose that?"

"That's not the point, Dad," she argued. "You know I don't want to see the town dissolved, but I'm a costume designer, not an accountant."

"We don't need an accountant," her father stated emphatically. "We need someone who has the time and the ability to organize a plan of action. We need someone with heart."

"Then you definitely don't want me. My heart's been kicked around so much this past year it's having a hard time just keeping *me* going," she said cynically.

He sat down beside her and took her hand between the two of his. "The best way to heal a troubled heart is to do for others, Sara. You know I've always believed that."

"I'm not sure I have anything to give."

"Of course you do. Everything happens for a reason. You didn't just come home because you had no place else to go."

Oh, but I did, she acknowledged silently, yet she couldn't admit that to her father.

"You needed to be with the people you love. The community of friends and relatives that has always been here for you," he continued.

She sighed. "And now that community needs me, right?"

"Yes." He smiled that wonderful smile, the one she took with her wherever she went, the one that said she could be anything she wanted to be because her father believed in her.

"I'm not the right person to head up the committee, Dad."

"You know everyone in town as well as I do. Do you honestly think any of them will do a better job of rallying folks to fight this thing?"

She wanted to tell him she had no fight left in her. All of it had been used up in the bitter divorce that had made her life miserable for the past year and a half. But he was looking at her with so much confidence in the twinkle in his eye that she couldn't disappoint him.

"Dad, I know this is important to you, but I honestly don't know if anything can be done to save the town."

That brought a sigh from her mother. "No one's expecting one person to come up with a solution, Sara. That's why you have a committee...and the support of the entire town."

"Yeah, all 272 of them," Sara quipped.

Her sarcasm produced a clicking of her mother's tongue. "They're good people. Not fancy-shmancy people like you knew in New York, but good, honest, hard-working people."

"I know, Mom," she agreed in a conciliatory tone. "I wasn't implying they're not. It's just that I don't know how we can do anything that's going to change the fact that the town has no income to keep it running."

Her father stood and looked down at her, a stern look

in his eye. She knew that look well. "I've never known you to be a quitter, Sara."

That look had its desired effect. It stirred something inside her that made her want to prove to him she wasn't someone who gave up without a fight.

"If something isn't done, Christmas could vanish," her father warned. "I don't know about you, but I don't want to someday pick up a road map and discover there's no longer a Christmas, Minnesota, on it."

She looked into his eyes and saw the plea of a man who had spent all fifty-seven years of his life in the small town. Fear, sadness, uncertainty—it was all there on his face and in his tone of voice. And rightly so. He had spent his life working as the postmaster of the small town, serving the people he loved. If the town were to disincorporate and merge with Denville, he'd lose not only his job, but also his identity.

And then there was her mother—her life, too, was firmly rooted in Christmas. After raising her own children, she had opened her home to preschoolers, running a day-care center. Sara's sister and brother-in-law still farmed nearby, and her brother lived in Christmas even though he taught school in Alexandria, some thirty-five miles away. She was the only one in her family who had left the small farming community for the bright lights of the city.

"Put your coat on, dear, and Dad and I will walk you home," her mother said as the last of the townsfolk leaving the hall called out to her father to lock up. "You know, your father has a point, Sara. This project will give you something to occupy your time. It'll help you adjust to living here."

And Sara knew it was going to be an adjustment. After spending the past six years traveling with a Broadway theater company that played the largest cities in the United States, she expected life in Christmas would definitely be an adjustment.

"It'll also help you become a part of the community again. If you're going to stay, you need to be involved," her mother added.

If she were going to stay. That was the big question.

Maybe her parents were right. Getting involved with the plans to save Christmas might just be what she needed to make her feel like her old self again. Except the mayor and everyone else expected her to solve the financial crisis confronting the town. What they didn't realize was that she had her own financial crisis, thanks to her ex.

She was broke; the town was broke. Some season to be jolly.

As they stepped outside, snow was falling. What once was a main street filled with lit storefronts was now in darkness. Only the street lamps and the lights from Fritz's service station lit the way.

"I think this is the first time I've ever seen the town without the usual Christmas decorations," Sara remarked as they walked home.

"It somehow didn't seem right spending the money on extras when we can't make the necessary bills," her father responded.

"It's that bad?" Sara asked.

He nodded grimly. "Every time it snows Buzz Gustafson has to plow, and we've already had him out six times."

"Five," his wife corrected him.

"But it doesn't seem like Christmas without the lights," Sara noted.

"You should see Alice Gibson's yard," her mother

said. "When she found out trimming Main Street was out, she decided to go all out and make her place the attraction in town. That's how she broke her foot— hanging the lights on the roof. Stepped on it wrong coming down the ladder."

"She'd be a good one to get on your committee," her father suggested. "At the last council meeting she said she'd fight tooth and nail to save the town. Course, that was before she broke her foot."

"She's not going to be around, is she? I thought she always goes to California in December to be with her family," Sara remarked.

"Not this year. She said she can't leave when the fate of Christmas is unresolved. Joe and Nikki are coming here."

That stopped Sara in her tracks. "Joe Gibson's coming home?"

"Is there a reason why he shouldn't be?" her father asked.

"He hasn't been back in ten years. Why now?" Sara answered.

"Because he doesn't want his mother to be alone at Christmas, although from what Alice tells me she thinks he's going to try to convince her to go back to California with him," her mother added. "I, for one, am glad he's going to be here."

Joe Gibson in Christmas. It was something Sara had thought she'd never see again. When he had left ten years ago, he had told her he was never coming back. Just the mention of his name sent a rush of memories through Sara's mind. She didn't want any of them there.

"Are you coming, dear?" her mother asked when she still hadn't moved.

Sara got into step beside them. "I bet he doesn't come," she remarked.

"Of course he'll come," her mother said in her typical Pollyanna I-see-good-in-everyone way. "I know you never thought much of Joe, but he's turned out to be a fine young man. Look at how good he is to Alice. He sends her plane tickets and pays all of her expenses so that she can go out to California every year."

"That's only because he doesn't want to come here," Sara said cynically. "It's easy to give money when you have lots of it. Time is something else."

"He's not had an easy life, Sara." Her mother's voice held a bit of a reprimand in it. "You know he was troubled as a teenager, and then to lose his wife in such a tragic way." She sighed in sympathy. "I'm sure Alice is very proud of the way he's turned his life around."

"If you don't mind, I'd rather not talk about Joe Gibson," Sara snapped a bit testily, which only drew curious looks from her parents. "Right now I have more important things on my mind. Like saving Christmas."

However, later that night it wasn't thoughts of how to raise the money to save the tiny town that kept her awake. Rather it was one seventeen-year-old boy who had kidnapped the prom queen. Joe Gibson had caused nothing but trouble for Sara since the day he had moved to town. He had made no secret of the fact that he wanted her to be his girl and had gone to great lengths to let everyone know—by kidnapping her from the prom.

No matter how hard Sara tried to forget what it had been like to be Joe Gibson's girl for one night, she couldn't. That's because it had been too good to forget. They had drunk strawberry wine and danced and kissed…forgetting all about the other thirty-one kids left back at the high-school gym. Forgetting all about her date—her steady boyfriend of two years.

Her behavior had been highly inappropriate that night, or so the senior-class adviser had said the following day when she had returned to help clean up after the prom. She had warned Sara of the problems a guy like Joe could bring to her life. Despite the fact that the senior-class adviser was her steady boyfriend's sister and had an ulterior motive for the warning, Sara knew what she said was true. There really was only one option for Sara. Stay away from Joe.

And she did. Immediately after graduation he left for California. She stayed in Christmas, commuting to the junior college in Alex. It hadn't taken him long to forget about her. Before Sara could even finish one semester, Joe had found someone else. Any doubts she had that she made the right decision regarding Joe disappeared when she heard the rumor that he had gotten a California girl pregnant.

Joe never contacted Sara again. Any news she had of him came from her mother, who was friends with Alice Gibson. The rumor proved to be true when Alice announced that Joe had married before even finishing his freshman year.

Who his wife was or what she looked like, Sara never knew. She was just a name Sara occasionally heard Alice speak. Angela Gibson.

That was because Joe never brought his family to Christmas. He never came home for the holidays, not even after his wife had died. Sara knew Joe never really considered Christmas home.

So why, after ten years, was he returning to the small town? It was true that his mother had a broken foot, but with her walking cast she managed to get around quite well. Maybe he was coming to gloat over the financial problems they'd been having. To take great pleasure in the town's misery.

Not that it mattered. Whatever Joe Gibson did was no concern to her. Maybe it wasn't such a bad idea that she would be involved with the Saving Christmas project. At least she wouldn't have to worry about running into him. If there's one thing he wouldn't care about, it was saving a town from which all he had ever wanted to do was run.

December 15, 4:30 p.m.

"ARE WE ALMOST THERE YET?" an impatient Nikki asked her father as his rented sport-utility vehicle ate up the miles on the rural highway.

"We're getting close," Joe Gibson answered, feeling the same restlessness as his daughter.

"Can't you drive faster? The speed limit is fifty-five and you're only doing fifty," Nikki said, leaning over to glimpse at the speedometer.

"Fifty-five is for when the roads are dry. There are still slick spots because of the snow," he retorted. That simply produced another impatient sigh from his daughter.

Ever since she had caught her first glimpse of snow, Nikki had been wiggling around in her seat, eager to reach her grandmother's so that she could make a snowman. Two days after he had told his mother that he and Nikki would be coming, a package had arrived from Minnesota. In it were a pair of shiny yellow insulated boots, a purple ski jacket with matching bib pants, a purple fleece headband and a pair of thick hand-knitted mittens—all for Nikki. Everything had been packed in a carry-on that Joe had stored in the overhead compartment of the plane.

The minute they had touched ground and Nikki had seen the mounds of snow, she had insisted on putting on the outdoor gear. Now she sat beside him, the nylon ski pants swishing every time she shifted her in seat—which was often.

"I wish you'd hurry. It's going to be so late by the time we get there that I won't be able to play outside," she grumbled as he slowed for a curve in the road.

"It's not my fault that your grandmother lives in the boonies," he grumbled right back.

Nikki wrinkled her nose. "What's the boonies?"

"Short for *boondocks*. It means a remote place. You know, far away from the city."

"Cool. I'm going to the boonies, I'm going to the boonies," she sang repeatedly until she was interrupted.

Joe said, "All right, cut it." He wondered if every kid could make a song out of a phrase or if it was just his particular kid.

There was more wiggling, more nylon swishing and another sigh.

"Look behind us. There's a beautiful sunset," he told her as he caught a glimpse of gold in his rearview mirror.

"Does that mean there'll be stars tonight?"

"The sky's clear. There should be."

"Grandma said she's got a bench out back where she sits to look at them. She likes stars, too."

"Well, don't expect Grandma to be out in this cold weather, especially not with her broken foot."

"She's not gonna be in a wheelchair, is she?"

"No. She does have trouble walking, though, and she

probably won't be able to get a boot on over her cast, which is another good reason why she should come home with us.'' It was one of many reasons he had put on a mental list, ready to do battle with his mother.

"Then who'll go with me when I play outside?''

"There are probably other kids in town, but you don't really need anyone, do you?''

"You never let me play outside by myself at home. You said it isn't safe.''

"That's because there are millions of people around L.A., nearly all of them strangers. In Christmas, there's only a couple of hundred and everybody knows everybody else.''

"So they know when someone commits a crime?''

He chuckled. "There isn't any crime in Christmas. They don't even have a cop.''

"Really?'' she asked in exaggerated disbelief.

"Don't need one. If there's any trouble, they call the sheriff over from Denville.''

"No wonder Grandma likes it there,'' she said thoughtfully. "It sounds like a nice place.''

Nice was not the adjective that came to mind in Joe's memory whenever he thought of the town. Cliquish. Boring. Close minded. They were more like it.

No, Christmas hadn't been a very nice experience for him. He had lived their sixteen months and two days, which was sixteen months and two days too long as far as he was concerned.

Now he was going back and he felt the familiar knot in his stomach—the one that had been his constant companion when he had been a teenager in Christmas. No sixteen-year-old wanted to transfer school in the middle of his junior year. What was even worse was having to leave a metropolitan area like Minneapolis with its malls and movie theaters and dance clubs to go to a town where the only light shining at night came from a pop machine and the entire population was smaller than the number of students in his graduating class at Southwest High.

His mother often told him he never gave the town much of a chance. She insisted that he had made up his mind he wasn't going to fit in before the first person in Christmas ever said hello to him.

Not that it mattered. That was all in the past. He was no longer a teenager and he didn't need to fit in anywhere. He was happy being a Californian and he wasn't going to stay one minute longer in the small town than was necessary to get his mother packed up and on a plane flying west.

"Look! There's a star over there!" Nikki said, sitting up straight in her seat. "See it? It's on the water tower. It's huge."

Joe saw the white lights in the shape of a star atop the familiar landmark. "We're here. That's Christmas, Nikki."

"Awesome! They've got a giant star!" she said, excitement in her voice.

Joe turned left onto the county road that bisected the highway. As if ten years hadn't passed, he felt like a teenager as he cruised down Main Street. It hadn't changed much at all, except familiar storefronts no longer boasted window displays but stood empty.

"How come there aren't any lights on?" Nikki asked as he drove through the business district.

"They roll up the sidewalks here at five o'clock." Seeing the puzzled look on his daughter's face, he quickly added, "That means they close the shops."

"There's someone over there putting a wreath up on that lamppost."

Joe's gaze followed the direction of Nikki's finger, and he saw a slender figure on a ladder wearing a hooded green parka, jeans and a pair of men's boots. He had a huge wreath in one hand, a length of wire in the other. Joe slowed, wondering if he should offer his help. It was obvious the man was struggling to get the oversize wreath attached to the pole. Nikki voiced the sentiments he was feeling.

"That guy looks like he needs help, Dad."

Joe noticed that the man was moving the wreath up and down on the post, getting the opinion of a second party across the street. It was only as he pulled up next to the curb that he saw the "second party" was none other than his mother.

"Dad, is that Grandma?" Nikki's disbelief was nearly as great as his.

Joe parked the sport-utility vehicle and climbed out, slamming his door with a thud.

"Ma, what are you doing out here?"

"Joe. Hi!" his mother called out from across the street. "We're putting up the Christmas decorations. It looks great right there, Sara," she hollered to the figure on the ladder.

"Sara?" Joe repeated, looking up at the person on the ladder.

As if suddenly aware of him standing below, Sara glanced down and Joe squinted. "Sara Richards?" He could hardly believe that the person on the ladder was the girl he had been in love with as a teenager.

A look of recognition flashed in her eyes only briefly, then she turned her attention back to the project at hand.

"I'm going to tie it right here," she shouted to his mother.

"It looks good. Go ahead and do it," his mother shouted back from across the street.

Joe moved closer to the lamppost. "Come down and let me do that," he said irritably, annoyed that his heart had pumped faster at the realization that it was Sara Richards on the ladder.

"I can't let go or it'll fall," she called down to him.

"I said come down and let me do it," he repeated.

"And I told you if I let go it'll fall. I can get it," she said in a tone that only annoyed him further. It was an ungrateful rejection of his offer.

So he climbed up the ladder and reached around her to secure the wreath in place with the wire. As he did, he realized that despite the bulkiness of the jacket, she was still a tiny little thing. Balanced precariously on the ladder, they each needed to work carefully so as not to knock the other one off. At one point he felt her hot breath against his cold cheek, and something stirred inside him. Even wearing a man's jacket she was feminine.

"Are you nuts, Sara?" he demanded, annoyed that his body was responding to her nearness.

"You're the one who's nuts. Climbing up on this ladder when there's barely room for one," she retorted. "We'll be lucky if we both don't fall and break our necks."

Whether it was fate or their combined weight, the ladder tipped to one side, sending the two of them sailing through the air. Joe landed flat on his back in a snowbank with Sara facedown on top of him.

It was at that moment that Joe knew nothing had changed between them.

He still wanted Sara Richards.

Chapter Two

For a moment Sara was too stunned to move. Then she realized she was on top of Joe Gibson. Actually, sprawled all over him would have been a better description. She didn't know which was more awkward—lying on top of him or trying to get off of him. When she tried to move, she knew it was the latter.

"Just terrific," Joe drawled with heavy sarcasm.

"I told you I didn't need any help," she said as she struggled to get up out of the snow. She felt the solid muscles of his chest, and a tiny chill traveled through her. She pretended it was because she had snow up her sleeves...which was true. She had snow in several places where it didn't belong, but she hardly noticed it. She was too conscious of the warm body beneath her.

"Dad, are you all right?"

The sound of a girl's voice had Sara looking up at the child standing over them. Sara's first thought was that she looked nothing like Joe. Whereas he was dark haired with an olive complexion, she was blond and fair. Sara's second thought was that Joe's wife had been a beautiful woman, for this child was lovely.

"I'll be fine once I get out of this cold," Joe grumbled, causing Sara to realize that he wouldn't be able to get up until she had disentangled herself from him.

The boots she had borrowed from her father now felt about six sizes too big for her as she tried to plant them on the ground. And the hood on her father's jacket had fallen back, revealing to all the world—and Joe Gibson—her limp hair. Alice had said her son wouldn't be home until later that night. Yet here he was, flat on his back in a suede jacket, gray dress slacks and a pair of black shiny shoes.

Sara finally scrambled to her feet and offered him a hand. He didn't take it, but sat forward, grimacing as he cleared a clump of snow away from the collar of his jacket. Then he attempted to stand, but quickly lost his balance. Sara and Nikki both helped him to his feet, providing him with an anchor for support.

"Good grief, Joe, where are your boots?" his mother said as she hobbled toward him on her crutches.

"Hi, Grandma." Nikki ran over and threw her arms around the older woman's waist.

Alice returned the affectionate squeeze. "Oh, it's so good to see you!"

"Thanks for sending me my snowsuit. It fits. See?" She did a pirouette for her grandmother.

"Yes, it does and I'm glad you wore it. Too bad your father didn't wear his winter clothes. He wouldn't be so cold," she said, tempering her criticism with a smile. She gave her son a hug and said, "I'm glad to see you made it without any problems. The roads have been a little slick in the area."

"So what else is new?" he barked.

As she released him she clicked her tongue and said, "No wonder you're cold. No boots, no gloves and no hat. And you, a native Minnesotan."

"Don't remind me," he muttered under his breath. But Sara heard.

Alice smiled indulgently as if he were a recalcitrant child. She turned to Sara and said, "This is my granddaughter, Nikki. Nikki, meet Sara Richards. She and your father went to school together."

It was only when Nikki smiled at her that Sara saw that she was truly Joe Gibson's daughter. It was there in the grin that lit eyes as blue as her father's.

"Hi, Sara." She extended a mittened hand.

"Hi, Nikki." Sara grasped the fingers hidden beneath the knitted mittens and looked into eyes fresh and innocent. There was something in the young girl's face that touched her heart—and it had nothing to do with the fact that she was Joe Gibson's daughter.

"Mother, what are you doing outside when the sidewalks are slippery?" Joe said irritably. "You've got a broken foot."

"We're saving Christmas," Alice Gibson answered.

"Saving Christmas from what?" he asked.

"From dissolving," his mother replied with a hint of impatience. "I told you about the trouble we've been having here. There's no money to pay for any services."

She turned to Nikki and said, "If something isn't done, we're going to disappear right off the map."

"You mean there won't be a Christmas anymore?" the nine-year-old asked.

"Not in Minnesota," Alice answered grimly.

"I don't think the situation's quite that bad, Mother," Joe stated. "Those rumors have circulated for years. There's always a shortage of money...people keep moving away...it doesn't mean the town is on its last gasp."

"Oh, but it is!" Alice pointed out with indignation. "We only have until end of the month. There are loan payments to be made, employees needing to be paid. This town is in debt, Joe, and something needs to be done by New Year's Eve or we're history. We'll become part of Denville."

Joe looked at Sara. "You really only have until the end of the year?"

She nodded grimly. "Your mother's right, Joe."

Alice was quick to put the blame where she felt it belonged. "It's all Chester Duggan's fault. He fell behind in paying the Stable's sales taxes, and you know what happens if the state doesn't get their money. They close you down."

Sara saw Joe glance across the street to the Stable, the only bar in town. As a teenager he had worked there, cleaning up the place after hours. She wondered if he was remembering just what had happened there ten years ago on the night of the prom. When his eyes met hers, she knew that he was and she felt her body warm.

"Once he was forced to close, we lost our source of revenue," Alice added. "The bulk of the town's budget comes from the money he pays for his liquor license."

"So how is hanging a wreath from a lamppost going to save Christmas?" Joe asked.

"It's all part of a plan," his mother answered smugly. "Sara, why don't you come back to the house and tell Joe all about it?"

Being in the same room with Joe was not where Sara wanted to be. "I would, but I'd better check to see how the advertising campaign is coming along."

"That's a good idea. We don't want to miss the newspaper deadlines." She turned to Joe and Nikki and

said, "Sara's organized a marvelous festival. Wait until
you hear about it."

The frown lines were back on Joe's face. "Mom,
why don't you take Nikki and wait for me in the car?"

As mother and granddaughter headed back to the
sport-utility vehicle, Sara heard Alice say, "Oh, I'm so
glad you came to see me. We're going to have so much
fun."

Sara could tell by Joe's face that fun was the last
thing on his mind. He had the same look in his eyes
that had been there the last time she had seen him. The
night she had told him that she was glad he was leaving
town because all he was doing was making her life miserable.

She swallowed back the memories and reminded herself that she was no longer a seventeen-year-old girl but
an adult woman who would be intimidated by no man.
That didn't stop her from wanting to turn around and
run away from his scrutiny.

"I thought you worked in New York." There was no
warmth in his words. "What are you doing back here?"

"Some of us have roots, Joe," she answered, knowing perfectly well that it was a blow below the belt. It
wasn't his fault that Alice Gibson hadn't found hers
until he was almost seventeen.

"You *wanted* to come back here?" His eyebrows
lifted in disbelief.

"Yes, I did." She raised her chin, trying not to give
him the tiniest inkling that it wasn't exactly the truth.
"Dullness is in the eyes of the beholder, Joe…or maybe
you haven't figured that out yet."

He looked around with a cynical eye. "In case you
haven't noticed, Sara, there's nothing left here but a gas
station, an empty bar and the post office."

"We may not have all the sparkle and glitter of a place like L.A., but we have something that isn't very easy to find in the city. Good people who care about what happens to their neighbors. People who are willing to trade a few conveniences for a sense of community you find in a town this size. People who look out for each other..."

"People who are judgmental and narrow-minded," he finished for her. "Don't forget to add *that* to your recruiting brochure."

Sara was surprised by the bitterness is his voice. She had thought that maybe after ten years his attitude toward Christmas might have changed. It hadn't, which only proved that she had been right about him. The only reason why he had sent his mother all those plane tickets was that he didn't want to have to come here to visit her.

She turned away from him and bent to pick up the ladder. "I'm going home. Even if you don't want to be here, at least try to act as if you do for your mother's sake," she advised.

"Let me help with you that."

He tried to take the ladder from her, but she refused to let go. "I can manage without your help."

They played tug-of-war with the rungs. "Will you quit being so stubborn and let me put it in the back of the Explorer?"

"No, I will not. I live one block away. I can manage," she stated firmly.

He finally let go, causing Sara to nearly lose her balance. "All right. Forget I even offered."

"You're easily forgotten," she retorted. Another lie.

He winced, as if the words had hurt him. Which Sara knew was ridiculous. Not once since he'd left had he tried to contact her. *She* was the one who had been easy to forget.

"I don't know what kind of a plan you have to save the town from disincorporation, but it's no longer going to include my mother," he stated firmly. "She has a broken foot, in case you hadn't noticed."

"And a healthy mind which she can make up for herself," Sara tossed back at him.

The way his eyes darkened sent a tremor of pleasure through her. It had been more than ten years since they had sparred verbally, and she realized that although she and Paul had fought like crazy, their fights had left her feeling drained. Not so with Joe. It was just the opposite. She felt alive exchanging words with him.

She didn't want to watch him walk away. She wanted to take the ladder and stomp away without so much as a goodbye or a glance in his direction. But she couldn't. She stood on the sidewalk, the ladder slung over her arm, watching until he climbed into the car.

As the Explorer pulled away from the curb, Alice rolled down the window and called out, "We'll see you tomorrow, Sara."

She couldn't see Joe's face, but she could imagine the scowl his mother's words produced. Poor Alice. She actually thought that she'd be able to get her son to help with the Saving Christmas campaign.

Joe Gibson wanted nothing to do with anything or anyone in the town. It might as well be ten years ago. Nothing had changed.

The only difference was now Joe didn't want Sara, either.

NIKKI'S EXUBERANCE COULDN'T be contained when Joe turned onto Second Street and his mother announced,

"There it is. That's Grandma's house with all the lights on it."

"Oh, my gosh! Grandma, it's beautiful!" Nikki fumbled impatiently with her seat belt in her haste to get out of the vehicle.

As soon as Joe had stopped beside the curb, she was out the door. "You've got Mickey and Minnie and Pluto and Goofy and...." She ran out of breath naming all of the lighted plastic figures on the lawn. "And a nativity scene." She knelt down beside the tiny manger. "I've never seen anything like this."

"That's why you came to Grandma's house for Christmas."

Irritation ricocheted through Joe. He hadn't come to spend the holidays here and he wished his mother had told him the truth about her injury. She had led him to believe she was having trouble walking, yet she was out in the snow hobbling about, using the crutches as if they were made for emphasizing her words, not supporting her lame foot. She was certainly able to climb aboard an airplane and fly to California.

He unloaded the luggage while Nikki and his mother continued their tour of the lighted displays in the yard. As much as Joe hated to admit it, his mother had done a remarkable job of decorating the house.

"Don't forget to look up." He heard her direct Nikki's attention to the roof, where a Santa sat in a sleigh pulled by plastic reindeer.

"Awesome! How did you get them up there?" Nikki wanted to know.

"Oh, your grandma is one smart lady. All it takes is a little bit of ingenuity and a whole lot of determination," she answered.

"What's ingenuity?" Nikki asked.

"Cleverness," Alice replied.

Joe came up behind his mother and quietly said, "As in telling your son you can't walk on your foot because it's in a cast?"

She turned around to face him. "It is in a cast. It's a walking cast."

"This is so neat!" Nikki was apparently unaware of the undercurrent in their conversation. "I could stay out here all night and never get tired of looking at it. Can I stay outside for a little while longer, Daddy?"

But Alice answered for him. "There will be plenty of time for you to play outside after dinner. First I want you to come inside so Grandma can make you something to eat and you can tell me all the things that have been happening since I last saw you."

She led Nikki up the porch steps to the front door, where she said, "Open the door for Grandma, will you?"

"Sure." She pulled off a mitten and extended her palm. "Give me the key."

"There's no need to lock your doors in Christmas, Nikki. Everyone looks out for everyone else here," Alice said as she ushered them inside. "It's a lovely place to live."

"If you like living in a fishbowl," Joe added under his breath. He didn't intend for Nikki to hear, but she did.

"Why is it like living in a fishbowl?" she asked with the naiveté of youth.

"What your father means is that sometimes when you live in a place where everyone knows everyone else, you sometimes feel like a fish behind glass. People know what you're doing most of the time," her grandmother answered.

"And is that bad?" Nikki wanted to know.

"I guess it depends on whether or not you're trying to hide anything," she answered, slanting Joe a glance.

Again he felt that surge of impatience. "Where should I put the suitcases?" he asked his mother, determined to change the subject.

"Take them upstairs. I'm putting you in your old room, and Nikki's going to share mine." She looked at Nikki and said, "Grandma borrowed a roll-away bed from Mrs. Swenson up the block. I put it right next to the window so you can look at the stars at night."

"Oh, Grandma, thank you so much!" Nikki was just about to race up the stairs when she noticed the balsam in the living room. "It smells good in here. Is that a real tree?"

"Chopped it down myself. Well, I had a little help," she admitted, plugging in the string of lights dangling near the floor.

"Cool! Where'd you get all these neat ornaments?" Nikki asked, fingering a tiny angel Joe recognized as having been in his mother's collection ever since he could remember.

"They're all old," Alice replied, "but they each have special meaning to me. Your grandfather bought me that one the year your great-grandmother died. He told me she was an angel, and every time I looked at that ornament I would think of her. And you know what? I do."

"I've never seen so many different kinds on one tree," Nikki remarked as her eyes scanned the branches.

"There's a story behind each one. After dinner we'll have a closer look, but first you should go upstairs and get settled in." She gave her a gentle nudge toward the stairs.

"Aren't you coming, Dad?" Nikki paused on the bottom step.

"In a minute. You go on up and I'll be right there," Joe answered. "It's the first room on the right."

As soon as his daughter had started up the stairs, Joe turned to his mother. "I thought I told you not to put a tree up. It's just one more thing for us to have to deal with before we pack you up."

"You're not packing me up," she informed him in no uncertain terms.

"Mom, we want you to spend Christmas with us."

"So stay here with me and we'll spend Christmas together."

"Nikki wants to be in Manhattan Beach with her cousins."

"Nikki does?"

"Yes, she does. I hope you're not going to fight me on this," he said on a sigh.

"There's nothing to fight about. I'm not going to California," was all his mother said before heading for the kitchen.

Joe knew there was no point in arguing with her at the moment so he carried the luggage up the stairs to the second floor. The house was small, the floors squeaked and the years slipped away, making him feel as if were once again the boy who sought solace in the one place he could call his own. His room.

As he stepped inside and turned on the light, it looked just as it had the day he had left it. The same blue plaid bedspread covered the twin bed, and the braided area rug sat in the middle of the floor, hiding the worn spots in the linoleum. An old metal desk his mother had found at a flea market sat next to the window with a bookshelf made out of bricks and old wood planks beside it. The only other furniture in the room was a wooden dresser that he had called his Viking chest. Painted a bright purple, it was the ugliest chest of drawers he had ever seen. His mother had picked it up at a garage sale for his thirteenth birthday. He had hated it until a couple of his friends had seen it and told him how lucky he was to have a dresser painted the same color as the local football team wore.

The room smelled of lemon, and he knew his mother, as usual, had polished all the woodwork. Although he hadn't used the room in over ten years, he would have bet money that it was dusted and polished on a regular basis. That's the way his mother was, always expecting he'd come back for a visit.

He opened the closet and saw his navy blue graduation gown on a hanger. Next to it was his old leather bomber jacket. He remembered how upset his mother had been when she had given him money to buy a parka and he had come home with what she called a biker jacket. He smiled to himself. He had felt so cool wearing the smooth leather and he knew all the kids in school had envied him.

On the floor of the closet was a pair of hockey skates. Christmas hadn't been big enough to have a hockey team. Not that it would have mattered if it had been. He hadn't been the jock type in high school.

Next to them was a pair of Sorel boots—not that he had ever worn them. He would have lost his reputation for being the coolest guy in school if had put on a pair of snow boots.

He glanced up at the shelf and saw a box, but before he could reach up to see what was inside, Nikki was behind him.

"Dad! Quick! You've got to come see what Grandma

has in her room.'' She tugged on his hand until he followed her across the hall. ''Look! It's a water bed! And look at this mirror.'' She stood in front of a full-length Cheval mirror ornately trimmed in gold. Then she moved over to the dresser, which housed a menagerie of miniature crystal animals. ''I've never seen so many beautiful little things. Look how they sparkle. Isn't Grandma cool?''

The subject of their conversation entered the room saying, ''What makes Grandma so cool?''

Nikki spread her arms wide. ''All of this. Your bed, the mirror, those teeny-weeny animals on your dresser.''

''They're Austrian crystal, Nikki. Would you like to take a few back with you?''

''You'd let me?'' Her eyes widened at the thought.

''Of course.''

''Oh, but I don't know which ones I'd pick.''

''You don't need to worry about that now. You'll have plenty of time to think about it. Christmas is still over a week away.''

''Mother, about the holidays,'' Joe began, but she quickly shushed him with a flap of her hand.

''Not now, dear. We can talk after dinner. If I don't get back downstairs, we'll be eating burned meat loaf.'' And before he could say another word, she hobbled out of the room and back down the stairs.

''Grandma's house is neat.'' Nikki's eyes were sparkling, causing Joe to feel a bit nervous. ''How come we never came to visit her before?''

He shrugged. ''It just seemed easier to have her come to California. We have more room at our place and it's not so cold.''

''I like it here. Everything inside is nice,'' she said,

admiring the assortment of perfume bottles and finger-nail polish on the vanity.

"Then I'm glad I brought you to see it. But you have to remember why we're here," he warned. "We want Grandma to come spend Christmas with us."

"What if she doesn't want to come back to California with us?"

"She'll want to," he said with more confidence than he was feeling.

"I hope so. It won't feel like Christmas without her." She climbed onto the roll-away bed to look out the window. "Grandma's really fun to be with."

Joe sat down beside her. "I'm sure she feels the same way about you."

"She gives me lots of hugs—just like Mom used to," she said, the sparkle in her eye chased away by a sadness Joe understood all too well. "When I'm with Grandma, it's easier not to miss Mom, especially at Christmastime."

Joe felt as if a cold hand reached inside his chest and squeezed his heart. He pulled his daughter closer to him, wrapping his arm around her childish frame. "You still miss your mother, don't you?"

She nodded solemnly.

"You miss her, too, don't you, Dad?"

"Of course I do. But part of her is still with me. You." He kissed her forehead. "You look a lot like her."

"Grandma says I have your nose."

Joe tapped the tip of her nose with his fingertip. "I think you have your own nose and a lovely nose it is."

She giggled.

"I don't want you to worry about Grandma not coming back with us, okay? I'm going to do whatever I can to make this the best Christmas ever.''

She scrambled over to the window. "It's awfully pretty here. So many of the houses have lights and decorations.'' She pressed her nose to the glass. "Look. I can make the window steam up.''

Joe got to his feet. "We'd better go downstairs. Grandma's making dinner. Are you hungry?''

"Yup, aren't you?''

"I'm always hungry for Grandma's cooking.''

She climbed off the bed and followed him out of the room. "See, that's another reason why we need her at Christmastime. You don't know how to make those little meatballs she always makes.''

"Don't worry. I think I know how to convince your grandmother she needs to come to California with us.''

"Good.'' She quickly changed the subject. "Do you think after dinner you could help me make a snowman outside? I told Lindsey and Shawna I'd build one and take a picture of it.''

"For you, Nik, anything's possible,'' he told her. And it was true. He would do whatever he could to make his daughter happy. Even if it meant a power struggle with his mother.

GRANDMA WAS RIGHT, Nikki decided as she lay in bed that night. She could see the stars right out the window. There were gazillions of them. Plus the giant star atop the water tower.

The minute she had first seen it, she had known that coming to Christmas was going to change her life. She wasn't sure how, but she knew that something important was going to happen. Of all the small towns they had driven through on their way from the airport, not one had had a giant star on its water tower.

Nikki saw it as a sign. For as long as she could remember, she had believed that all of her wishing on stars would someday pay off. Her Sunday-school teacher, Mrs. Bergstrom, had told her to be patient. That wishes took time to come true.

Well, she had been patient.

It hadn't always been that way. When she had first started wishing on the stars, things were different. After her mother died, Mrs. Bergstrom had told her that the one wish that would never come true was the one Nikki wanted the most—for her mother to leave heaven and return to earth. At six Nikki hadn't understood why it wasn't possible, especially not when they learned about miracles in Sunday school.

Mrs. Bergstrom had said that someday she would wish for another special lady to come into her life. Someone who would make cookies with her and curl her hair and make her feel better when she cried because the girls at school didn't invite her to their birthday parties.

For a long time Nikki hadn't wanted to waste a wish on such a person. She had seen the ladies her father had dated, and none of them were anything at all like what she would want a stepmom to be. Thank goodness her father hadn't thought so, either.

Mrs. Bergstrom had said she didn't need to think about it, that everything happened in due time. Whatever due time meant. She had assured her that her wishes would change as she grew older.

Nikki didn't want to believe her. It just hadn't seemed right to want to wish for a stepmom. Instead she had wished that the women her father dated would get boring and stop dating him. And she had wished that her father would like to go shopping. And that he would like to play dolls. One time she had even wished that he would take her to get her ears pierced.

But although her dad was a pretty good dad and did most of the things she asked him to do, he couldn't do some of the stuff she really needed. Like go with her to the mother-daughter breakfast at church. Or French braid her hair. Or go in the bathroom with her at the mall.

As much as she hated to admit it, she needed some-one like Mrs. Bergstrom in her life. Only her Sunday-school teacher was too old. Her father would never fall in love with someone with gray hair. And of course there was the problem of *Mr.* Bergstrom.

No, she and her father needed to find someone around twenty-five. Someone pretty and smart who would know how to make her dad laugh and could show her how to do all the things girls were supposed to do.

That's why she was using those windows in the sky to speak to her mother. Because if anybody could help her it was her mom. She was right up there in the place where prayers were answered.

So the last thing she said before she fell asleep that night was, ''I think it's time, Mom. I'm ready for my Mrs. Bergstrom.''

Chapter Three

December 16, 12:01 a.m.

Sara rolled over and glanced at the digital clock. It was after midnight and she was still tossing and turning. Why had she eaten that fudge-swirl cheesecake with the raspberry sauce? It had refused to go quietly into her digestive system.

She pushed aside the down comforter and climbed out of bed. The wood floor was cold beneath her bare feet, and she hurried to find her slippers. As she headed for the kitchen, the house was in darkness except for the glow of the bathroom's night-light that sent a tiny beam into the hallway. She crept as quietly as she could past her parents' bedroom, her slippers barely making a sound as she moved.

Instead of the fluorescent overhead that hugged the kitchen ceiling, she turned on the light above the stove, then opened a cupboard. As she expected, on the second shelf was the bottle of antacid relief. She took two spoonfuls, grimaced, then washed it down with a glass of water. Just as she was about to return the bottle to the cupboard, the overhead light flickered into a bright luminescence that lit the entire kitchen.

"I thought I heard someone up," her mother said from the doorway.

"I'm sorry, Mom. I didn't mean to wake you."

She waved Sara's apology away with a flap of her hand. "I wasn't asleep, either. Too much going on at this time of year, I guess." She eyed the bottle of antacid liquid. "Tummy upset?"

"That cheesecake is sitting like a big rock in my stomach," Sara answered. "Make that a big angry rock."

"You shouldn't have had a second piece," her mother chastised her gently.

"I shouldn't have had any." She returned the bottle to the cupboard.

"What you need is a cup of chamomile tea." She gently moved Sara out of the way. "Sit and I'll make us both a cup."

Sara tried to protest. "Mom, you don't have to do that. You should be in bed. The kids come so early."

Again she gave Sara a gentle nudge toward the table. "I'm not *that* old that I can't stay up and have a cup of tea with my daughter. Go sit."

Sara did as she was instructed, her heart warming at the sight of her mother padding about the kitchen in her pink chenille robe. Except for a few additional lines around her eyes and a few extra pounds around her middle, her mother had changed little since the days when Sara had lived at home.

"Are you sure it's the cheesecake keeping you awake, or is it something else?" her mother asked as she filled the teakettle with water.

"What else would it be?"

"I thought maybe because you saw Joe Gibson this evening..." She trailed off, her eyes full of curiosity.

Sara chuckled sardonically. "The days of me losing sleep over Joe Gibson are over, Mom. I'm not seventeen anymore."

"I know that, but sometimes old memories can stir up emotions we thought were buried."

"Nothing like that happened when I saw him," she assured her mother, although it wasn't exactly the truth. Maybe she hadn't felt that schoolgirl-type attraction she'd had for him ten years ago, but she had definitely had a physical reaction to him. "Believe me, Mom, after what I've been through the past few years, a relationship with a man is the last thing on my mind."

"Well, there'd be no point in starting something up with Joe, would there? I mean, it's not like he's going to stay here," her mother said in a voice that sounded an awful lot to Sara like a warning. She slipped a faded green tea cozy over the teapot and pulled two china cups from the cabinet.

"This is one of the things I've missed most since you've been gone," her mother said wistfully. "Having tea late at night. When you were a teenager, I used to always wait up for you when you were out. Then we'd sit and have a cup of tea when you'd return. Remember?"

Sara smiled wistfully. "I do. You never fell asleep, no matter how late I was out—and sometimes it got to be pretty late."

"You never gave us any reason to worry."

Sara knew that wasn't true. There was one night when she hadn't come home at all. The night she had spent with Joe Gibson. It wasn't something she wanted to discuss with her mother. Besides, it was a memory better left forgotten.

Eugenia carried the teapot to the table and sat down.

"So tell me what's going to happen tomorrow to convert our town into a Victorian village?"

During the first meeting of the Saving Christmas committee, it had been decided that the townspeople would put all their efforts into a one-day fund-raiser. Sara knew that to draw visitors and nearby residents on a day like Christmas Eve, they needed to make their town truly special. They'd come up with a plan to turn the town into a Victorian village with something for everyone.

"We're transforming the Baker building into a market. We thought we'd put the crafts in there since Henry already has the tables in the back room." At one time the Baker building had housed a hardware store, but now like most of the other buildings in Christmas, it sat empty.

"Alice said she's bringing her granddaughter to help make the paper chains for the tree in the dining center," Eugenia commented as she poured each of them a cup of tea.

"She must have decided that before Joe arrived."

"Why would Joe's arrival change that?"

"Because he told me in no uncertain terms yesterday that his mother was not going to be a part of the campaign. So he certainly isn't going to allow his daughter to help."

A hint of a grin curved her mother's lips. "I can't imagine anyone telling Alice what to do, can you?"

"She is strong willed."

"Stubborn is what most people say."

"That's why she fits in with the rest of us, isn't it?" Sara teased. She was enjoying the quiet time with her mother. "I've missed this, too, Mom. And I want to thank you and Dad for letting me move home again."

"You don't need to thank us, Sara." She gave her hand a squeeze. "This is still your home. It always has been and it always will be."

"But you don't need an extra person underfoot."

"You're not underfoot," she insisted with a click of her tongue. "Now, no more of this talk. Tell me what Alice's granddaughter is like."

"Nikki? She's cute. Blond, blue eyed."

"Does she look like Joe?"

"Not really. Except when she smiles. Then the resemblance is there."

"What about Joe? Has he changed much since high school?"

"Maybe a few pounds heavier. His hair isn't as long as it was back then. Otherwise he's the same, I guess."

"Alice thinks she's going to be able to talk him into staying for Christmas."

Sara chuckled. "That's about as likely as Santa coming down the chimney."

"Well, I guess it's nothing we have to worry about, is it?" her mother stated pragmatically, then she padded off to bed, leaving Sara alone to wonder with whom Joe Gibson usually spent his holidays.

His wife had been dead three years. Certainly there was another woman in his life. After all, everyone in Christmas knew that Joe liked women. Or maybe it would have been more accurate to say women liked Joe. There hadn't been a single girl in her high-school class who hadn't dreamed of being in his arms.

But he hadn't dated any of the girls in town. No, the mighty Joe Gibson chose girls from Denville or Starbuck or Vargas or any other town that wasn't Christmas. Which Sara thought had only added to his appeal. The more he had made it clear that he wasn't interested in any of the girls at school, the more attractive he had become.

Seeing him tonight had brought back memories Sara had long forgotten. Of school days, of summer vacation, of the night they had spent together. For the first time in her life, she had been a bit of a rebel. She had danced, had had her first taste of strawberry wine and had discovered what it was to want a boy so badly she couldn't think of anything but being with him.

A schoolgirl crush. That's all it had been. Every girl had one. The only reason why hers had been on Joe Gibson was that he had been like forbidden fruit. Bad for her.

Well, she was no longer seventeen. She was beyond the stage of schoolgirl crushes and she wasn't interested in Joe Gibson.

So why couldn't she stop thinking about him?

JOE NEVER SLEPT WELL away from home. It was one of the reasons he hated traveling. That's why he was surprised when he awoke the following morning and discovered it was after nine. He had slept like a baby in the narrow twin bed. It had been a long time since he had had such a good night's rest.

After a quick shower, he headed downstairs, expecting to find Nikki and his mother already in the kitchen having breakfast. Instead he found a note scribbled in his mother's writing.

Went to help Sara at the Baker building. Coffee's in the thermos. Enjoy your morning.

Love,
Mom and Nikki.

Joe crumpled the note in his fist. So his mother was determined to keep working on the campaign to save Christmas. He should have known nothing he had said last night would change her mind. She was as stubborn as she had always been. And if it wasn't bad enough that she had gone straight back to help with the futile efforts to save the town, she had taken Nikki with her. Irritation had him ignoring the hunger pains in his stomach and reaching for his coat.

As he stepped out the back door, he was assaulted by a blast of cold air that stung his cheeks and changed his breath into a tiny white cloud. His mother was right. He should have come better prepared for the frigid temperatures, but he had forgotten just how nasty a Minnesota winter could be.

It all came rushing back, however, as he hit a slick spot on the walk and nearly careened into the Explorer. Cussing under his breath, he headed back into the house and up the creaky stairs to his room. He pulled open the closet door and grabbed the insulated boots in the corner. With a grimace he kicked off his shoes and put on the Sorels. Then he dug in his suitcase for the leather gloves he should have had in his jacket pockets yesterday.

Back into the cold he went on a mission to save his mother and daughter from wasting their time. Before he could rescue anyone, however, he needed to scrape the thick layer of frost covering the car's windows. By the time he had accomplished the task, he was angry at the whole state of Minnesota.

But mainly he was angry at Sara Richards. It was her fault that his mother wasn't home this morning. When it came to recruiting people to get involved in some hopeless project, there was no one better than Sara. In high school there had been a whole list of lost causes she had championed. Like the car wash she had organized to buy new uniforms for the football team. Or the bake sale she had orchestrated to fund a trip to St. Paul. And then there was the time she fought to make sure the senior class had a prom.

Unfortunately for Joe, that particular cause had not been lost. He had thought it was a stupid idea, trying to save the prom from extinction. He had never been one to attend dances, not even when he had been a city kid.

Then there was the matter of being on the outside looking in. His classmates had made it perfectly clear that he didn't belong anywhere near their social events.

The temptation to flout tradition—to live up to his reputation as the town's bad boy and wear a pair of jeans instead of a tux to the dance—had been great. To thumb his nose at all of those small-town people who thought he was a loser. To show the "in" kids that he didn't give a damn.

Instead he had come up with a better plan. Rather than annoy people with his presence at the dance, he'd take away the one person they all wanted to be there. The prom queen herself, Sara Richards.

Eleven years ago when his mother had dragged him kicking and screaming to Christmas, he had thought there would be no girl in town who could possibly attract his attention. He had been wrong. From the first day he had seen Sara, he hadn't been able to stop thinking about her.

Not even when he had discovered she was the most popular girl in school. Or that she had a reputation as the town's Goody Two-shoes. Or when she made it perfectly clear to him that she was Roger Colvin's steady girl.

He shouldn't have been attracted to her. She was nothing like the girls he usually dated, yet something about her tempted him to forget that she was the class president and he the class problem.

Maybe it was because she had never quit trying to help him fit in. When everybody else had given up on him, she had continued to ask him to be a part of the activities at school. She also understood Oscar Wilde.

That's why he had kidnapped her the night of the prom. Because no matter what Sara said about being Roger Colvin's girl, her heart didn't truly belong to him. How could it when Roger thought Oscar Wilde was a brand of wieners?

No, he and Sara had been soul mates. And he had proved it to her that night at the Stable. Or so he thought.

His body warmed at the memory of how they had nearly made love that night. Nearly. Because if there was one thing that had been true about Sara, it was that she *was* a good girl. Even though they had slept in each other's arms and declared their hearts were one, they had decided to wait to make their bodies one.

Remembering just how close they had come to being completely intimate caused Joe's body to react in a purely physical way. "Damn, you're not seventeen, Gibson," he chastised himself, hating the fact that the memory of what Sara had felt like in his arms could still arouse him and create an ache inside him.

Not that it should surprise him. It had been three years since Angela had died, and although there had been women in his life, it wasn't easy to have an intimate relationship when one was a single parent. And even without having to consider Nikki, he simply hadn't found a woman he wanted to take to bed.

No matter what his body tried to tell him, Sara Richards was not the one, either. Nor would she ever be, he told himself as he parked across the street from the Baker building.

As he stepped inside the old hardware store, the odor of paint was strong. Several heads turned his way, none of them belonging to his mother. All of the faces looked familiar, but there was only one he remembered. It belonged to his high-school math teacher.

"Well, Joe Gibson! If it isn't good to see you." A burly, enthusiastic hulk of a man came over to shake his hand, a welcoming grin on his face. "Your mother said you were back. How've you been?"

"I'm good, Mr. Hanson."

"You look great. I hear you're a stockbroker."

"Actually, I'm a market analyst," he said, giving the room a cursory look in hopes of finding his mother.

Sam Hanson whistled through his teeth. "There's gotta be a lot of stress in a job like that."

Joe smiled. "Probably no more than in trying to teach a bunch of teenagers the Pythagorean theorem."

"Didn't you hear? I'm not teaching anymore. When they merged Christmas High School with Denville and Vargas, I lost my job. I'm selling computers over in Alex now."

It shouldn't have surprised Joe. Talk of closing the schools had circulated when he had lived in Christmas. Most of the small towns around them had already merged their school districts by the time he left. Vaguely he remembered his mother mentioning the subject a few years back.

"Sounds like a suitable job for a math whiz," Joe said.

"I always said technology was the key to the future. We're taking a step back in time here today." Sam motioned toward the other men in the room who were busy painting and hanging garland throughout the room. "It's going to be quite a celebration."

"What is?"

"You know, the Victorian Christmas celebration. We weren't going to paint, but the place was looking a little shabby so we thought a fresh look would brighten things up. You have to make it appealing or the folks won't want to buy anything."

Curious, Joe asked, "What is it you want them to buy?"

"Crafts. This is going to be the gift shop, full of crafts. Wait until you see all the stuff the ladies have managed to find. If you care to help out, we've got more brushes in the back room." He looked at Joe expectantly.

"Actually, I was looking for my mother. Is she here?"

"She's up the block at the Stable. That's where they're going to serve the food."

Joe wrinkled his forehead. "I thought the Stable went out of business."

"Oh, it did, but Chester offered to let us use it while he tries to find a buyer. Of course we won't be able to serve any liquor, but that's probably a good thing. It's supposed to be a family celebration."

The more Joe heard the word *celebration,* the more skeptical he became. "Just when is this…er…celebration supposed to take place?"

"Christmas Eve day. So you can see, we have a lot of work to do in a short time."

"And I should let you get back to it," Joe said, reaching for the handle on the door.

"It certainly is good to see you, Joe. I expect we'll see more of each other, what with all the events that are planned," Sam said with a grin.

Joe didn't tell him that he had no intention of attending any event—planned or unplanned—in Christmas. He simply said, "You take care, Mr. Hanson."

"You, too, Joe. And welcome home."

Christmas wasn't home for Joe. It never had been. However, he knew there would be no point in telling that to his former teacher. So he just waved and headed up the block toward the Stable. Before he could reach the bar, he heard a woman's voice call out to him.

"Joe Gibson, you stop right there and give your auntie Jean a hug."

He turned around to see his mother's best friend, Jean Carson, standing beside a door that had the words Mother Goose Land painted on the glass. Her arms were spread, waiting for him to do as she commanded.

He had to stoop to give her a hug, as Jean was barely over five feet tall, but what she lacked in height she made up for in width.

"Oh my, it's been a long time," she declared affectionately, hugging him tighter than even his mother had done. Then she pushed him away, scrutinizing him closely. "Let me look at you. Oh, your mother is wrong! You haven't changed a bit...except maybe you've filled out." She pulled him by the hand into the shop. "It's too cold to be chitchatting on the street. Let's go inside and I'll show you what we've done with the place."

The "place" was a shop that had once been a beauty salon. Like the hardware store, it, too, had gone out of business as the town's population dwindled.

"We're making this place for kids. They can come in here, have some apple cider or hot chocolate and listen to Mother Goose stories," she explained, leading him over to a section of the store where a giant shoe had been painted on the wall.

Joe saw that all of the walls had been covered with paper murals of nursery-rhyme characters. "Someone's put a lot of work into this," he observed.

"Everyone in town has contributed in one way or another, but we owe most of it to Sara Richards. Without her, none of this would have been possible." She walked over to a countertop that had once been a beauty station but now served as a kitchen area. "Would you like a cup of hot chocolate? I'm giving the machine a trial run." She didn't wait for him to answer but filled a paper cup.

The aroma of the hot chocolate reminded Joe that he hadn't eaten any breakfast. "Smells good." He took a sip. "Tastes as good as it smells."

Her lips curved into a smile of satisfaction. "That's a load off my mind. Now come have a seat in the reading room and we can catch up."

"I'd like that, but I need to find Mom."

"She's probably at the Stable. She and Martha Wiggins are in charge of the food for this thing," Jean told him.

"Just what is this *thing*, Jean?"

"Didn't your mother tell you?"

"We haven't had much time to talk," he told her, not wanting to admit that his mother had refused to talk about the Saving Christmas campaign last night.

Jean bent down to reach for something beneath the counter. When she popped back up, she had a red flyer in her hand that she gave to Joe. "We're having a one-day festival, a sort of Victorian village, where people can get carriage rides, buy handcrafted items, hear some Christmas music, eat some holiday food."

"And you're planning to do it on Christmas Eve?"

"We figure we'll get a lot of travelers to stop on their way to their family gatherings. We're right off the main highway that goes to Alex."

Joe scanned the flyer in his hands. He could hardly believe it! *This* was Sara Richards's way to save the town?

"It seems like an awful lot of work for one day," he cautioned.

"It's a labor of love, Joe. Everyone in town knows how important it is. Why, what would happen to us if the town dissolved?" She answered her own question. "We'd lose everything that's meaningful to us."

Joe didn't have the heart to tell her that they had already lost everything that mattered—the businesses that kept the town alive.

"All of this planning and pitching in to help...well, it's been good for the town, Joe," Jean said earnestly. "United, we can get through this trouble we're facing. I'm so glad you came home to lend a hand."

But he hadn't. He drained the last of the hot chocolate. "Thanks for the cocoa."

"Oh, it is so good to have you back, Joe." She wrapped her chubby arms around him one more time. "You tell your mother I'm going to cook a pot roast and I expect the three of you to come to dinner tomorrow night. You hear?"

"I'll tell her," Joe replied dutifully, warmed by the

affection in the older woman's voice. He should have told her he wasn't back, that he hadn't come home to lend a hand with anything. But he couldn't.

Over the years Jean had been nothing but kind to him, always treating him like the son she never had. And he hadn't made it easy for her. Jean had been the one who had convinced his mother to move to Christmas, something Joe didn't appreciate at the time. But somehow his mother was comfortable in the close-knit community.

Just how comfortable was pointed out to him when he stepped into the Stable and saw a small group gathered around her.

"Hey, Dad."

Joe looked toward the bar and saw his daughter with a broom in her hand. Covering her jeans and sweatshirt was a white bartender's apron.

He walked toward her. "What are you doing?"

"I'm sweeping the floor," she stated the obvious, and continued on as if it were of the utmost importance that she do it well. Joe then walked over to his mother, who finally noticed his presence.

"You look a little owly. Didn't you make yourself any breakfast?" she asked him before turning to the other three women at the table and saying, "Joe always gets crabby if he doesn't eat breakfast."

"Why is Nikki working?" he demanded, her words making him even crabbier.

"Because I want to help save Christmas." It was Nikki who answered.

"There's nothing wrong with her pushing a broom around, Joe," his mother said in a condescending tone.

"I don't want her working in a bar," he stated in no uncertain terms.

The people around Alice cleared their throats, and she rose to her feet. "I better make you something to eat. You'll feel better if you get some food in your stomach," she said, walking toward the kitchen.

"I don't need food in my stomach to feel better. I need for you to forget about this futile plan to save Christmas."

"What does *futile* mean?" Nikki asked, pausing to lean on the tip of the broom.

"It means useless," her grandmother answered.

"Don't you want Christmas to be saved, Dad?"

Joe could feel more than one set of eyes on him awaiting his answer. "I think you'd better go back to the house with your grandma."

"But I'm not going back to the house, Joe," his mother said with an annoying calmness. "I have work to do."

"Then I'll take her back myself." Joe grabbed the broom from his daughter's fingers. She protested loudly.

"Dad! I don't want to go back."

He ignored her, untying the apron from around her neck.

"Dad, stop! What is wrong with you? I'm having fun helping. Everyone's real nice and they're going to do all sorts of fun stuff."

Joe realized that every eye in the place was staring at him. He could feel his face grow warm. What *was* wrong with him? He gently placed his hands around Nikki's waist and placed her on a bar stool.

"We had other plans for today, remember?" he said, sitting down beside her. "I was going to show you around the town."

"But Grandma promised Sara she'd get the food organized for the Victorian Christmas celebration," Nikki said. "Sara says we're going to make some of the foods they made in Victorian England. We're going to have puddings and cakes and truffles and all sorts of neat things." Her eyes grew wider as she spoke.

Sara. The mere mention of her name agitated Joe. As much as he hated to admit it, his mother was right. He should have had breakfast because right now he was feeling extremely crabby.

"So Sara does all the planning and leaves you to do all the work. Is that it?" he asked when he had glanced around and saw that she was nowhere in sight.

"Oh, Joe, that's not fair," Alice told him. "Sara's working very hard. See for yourself. She's in the walk-in cooler."

He certainly would see for himself. Having spent most of his senior year cleaning up and stocking shelves in the Stable, he knew his way around the bar. He didn't need anyone to tell him where the cooler was. He would find Sara.

Again, just thinking about her stirred emotions in him he didn't want disturbed. He slid off the bar stool and swept through the kitchen, past the grill, to the large metal door that normally was shut but today was slightly ajar.

The sight of Sara on the ladder, her blond curls bouncing as she scrubbed one of the shelves, sent a familiar tremor through him. He stepped into the cooler, pulling the door shut behind him.

The sound caused Sara to let out a tiny yelp of surprise.

"Good grief, Joe. What are you trying to do? Make me fall from a ladder a second time?"

Chapter Four

Sara didn't climb down the ladder. She wouldn't. Not for Joe Gibson. If he wanted to talk to her, he could do it standing beneath her. She continued scrubbing as if she didn't care whether he was there—which couldn't have been further from the truth. Just knowing he was in the vicinity made every hair on her body stand on end.

"What are you doing?"

"I'm cleaning the shelves." She dipped her sponge into the bucket and slopped a pool of water onto the smooth surface.

"Would you come down so I could talk to you." It was more of a command than a request.

"I can hear you just fine from where I am." She hated the way her voice suddenly sounded breathless.

"I prefer to look people in the eye when I talk, so unless you want me to join you on the ladder, I suggest you come down here," he said in a dangerously calm voice that made Sara's heart flutter.

She ignored his threat. "Quit wasting my time, Joe, and say whatever it is you have to say."

She heard boots clomp across the floor, then the ladder wiggled. When she looked down, he was on the first rung. "Get off this ladder!"

He continued to climb until he was one step below her, which—because of the difference in their heights—put his torso even with hers. The soft suede of his jacket brushed against her arms as he placed a hand on either side of her.

"You are even more stubborn than I remembered," he said next to her ear. His breath was warm against her hair, the clean, crisp scent of aftershave wafting tantalizingly around her.

"If we fall off this thing, they'll be no snowbank to cushion our fall," she warned, annoyed that he could stir her feminine senses.

"Then I suggest you don't move or we might both be lying down there with more than a few bumps and bruises."

She squirmed and the ladder wobbled. "See?" he said smugly.

"Joe, you get down off this ladder. Now!"

"Or you'll what? Scream?"

He had a point. What could she do? "Just get down and I'll come down, too. I promise."

He clicked his tongue. "I know how well you keep your promises, Sara."

So he hadn't forgotten what had happened between them ten years ago. Her body grew warm. "I'm twenty-eight, not seventeen, Joe," she said a bit impatiently, annoyed that his nearness should cause her heart to beat as if she were still a teenager and the object of his affection.

"You still look like the same Sara to me."

"I'm not. I've changed."

"You've filled out," he remarked, which sent a wave of heat through her.

"This is making me really nervous, Joe. Can we just got off this thing before we get into trouble?"

"I'm not seventeen anymore, either, Sara. Trouble doesn't follow me around."

"I believe you. Now can we get down?" she pleaded.

To her surprise, he climbed down the ladder. She followed, giving him a nasty look as she reached the floor.

"All right. Say what you have to say." She shoved her hands on her hips, trying to maintain a posture that would tell him she was not intimidated by his presence. Even though she was.

And with good reason. This morning he looked even more attractive than he had last night. In the dusky evening light she hadn't been able to see just how dark his eyes were. Or that he now had a tiny scar near his left eyebrow. Ten years had chased away the boyishness; replacing it was a maturity that was much sexier. A warm fuzzy feeling tingled inside Sara. But then he spoke, and any heat spreading through her body was chilled by his words.

"I don't want my mother in charge of making food for anyone. You're going to have to replace her because even if she thinks she's capable of getting the food organized, she's not going to be here for your celebration. She's going back to California to spend the holidays with me and my daughter."

"I don't know why you're telling me this, Joe. Shouldn't you be having this conversation with your mother?" she said smoothly.

She could see that she had irritated him. A pulse beat next to the tiny scar on his forehead. "I'm telling you because it's your fault that she's here working when she should be at home with a broken foot. Now, I don't know what it is you've told her that has guilted her into helping you with this scheme to save the town, but I want you to stop putting the pressure on her to stay.''

Anger pooled inside Sara. ''I haven't *guilted* her into doing anything! I'm only doing what she asked me to do…what the town asked me to do. And you have a lot of nerve coming in here and blaming me because your mother doesn't want to go with you to California, Joe Gibson.'' Any attempt to maintain her self-control vanished as she wagged her finger at him.

''That's my point. Her bags would be packed and she'd be ready to go this very minute if you hadn't roped her into this ridiculous scheme to save a town that's been dying for the past fifty years.''

She gasped. ''It's not dying! You look out front and up and down Main Street and you'll see a community that's come together and is working night and day to do whatever it takes to save their town.''

''You can't possibly make enough money off some little plan to sell cookies and pies to get this town out of debt,'' he said derisively.

''And how would you know what we can do? You haven't lived here in ten years. You know nothing about these people.''

''I know a ridiculous plan when I see one. Don't you feel the least bit guilty that you're making them work for nothing?''

''It's not for nothing!''

''You can't honestly think people are going to come here on Christmas Eve to attend some flea market.'' He stared at her in disbelief.

''Flea market?'' she repeated indignantly. ''It's a

Victorian Christmas village, and of course they'll come. People are sentimental when it comes to holidays and they're looking for new and different ways to celebrate.''

"They're not looking to spend time in a town that's about ready to fold. Your plan doesn't have a chance to succeed." His voice softened as he said, "People aren't going to come, Sara."

"Yes, they will. Have you forgotten about the field of dreams? No one thought it had a chance, either."

He laughed out loud. "We're not talking baseball here. Eating roasted chestnuts while listening to Mother Goose rhymes is not a national pastime. Sara, it's winter. The only travelers on the highway are going to be people in a hurry to get to their holiday celebrations."

She hated that he was stating all the doubts she herself had shared with the committee. Despite that fact, she managed to say, "I think you're wrong."

"Wrong or right, I'm telling you not to count on having my mother's—or my daughter's—help."

She didn't back away from him as he leaned closer to make his point. She stood her ground and said, "And I'm telling you that *if* your mother doesn't want to be a part of the celebration, she can tell me herself."

"She won't do that because she thinks if she backs out now she's letting you down."

She thrust her hands to her hips. "And just what is it you expect me to do, Joe? Go out there and tell her what? That we don't want her help?"

"You can tell her the truth. That this plan doesn't have a snowball's chance in hell and she'd be better off in California where she'd get the rest she needs to heal her foot."

"Maybe I should have the mayor call a town meeting," she drawled sarcastically. "That way I can make the announcement to everyone at once." She cleared her throat and acted as if she were addressing a large crowd. "Even though you're all putting your heart and soul into saving the town, we're going to scratch the Victorian Christmas plans because Joe Gibson, who hasn't lived here in ten years, thinks it's a waste of time."

Again the pulse in his temple throbbed and he tightened his mouth, as if trying to control his temper. "I don't care what you do as long as it doesn't involve my mother."

"Not even if it makes her happy?"

Before he could answer, Nikki popped her blond head inside the door. From the look on her face, Sara knew she had heard them arguing.

"Hi, Nikki. What's up?" she asked the child.

"Grandma says to tell you there's a man here with the turkeys," she answered, her eyes darting back and forth between Joe and Sara.

"Tell your grandma to have him leave them outside," Sara instructed her.

Nikki nodded and disappeared. Sara took advantage of the interruption to say, "You'll have to excuse me, Joe. I have to finish so we can get this cooler running. We have food that needs to be stored in here." She started back up the ladder, half expecting he'd say something to her.

He didn't. He simply turned around and walked away.

December 17, 10:30 a.m.

WITH ONLY FOURTEEN DAYS before the disincorporation deadline, Sara sat in the Stable putting the finishing touches on Jean's Mother Goose costume. Only her thoughts weren't on the Victorian Christmas celebration. They were on Joe Gibson. As hard as she tried not to think about him, she found he was a much more intriguing subject than the town's fiscal woes.

She didn't want to be curious about him, but she couldn't help but wonder what his life was like in California. Was he involved with anyone special? Was that the reason he didn't want to spend the holidays in Christmas? Because there was a woman in L.A. awaiting his return?

When the bell on the door tinkled, indicating someone had come into the bar, she glanced up, hoping that it might be Joe. It was his daughter.

"Hi, Sara. Grandma says to tell you she'll be next door talking to Auntie Jean if you need her." She plopped down onto a chair next to Sara. "Is that your dog outside the front door?"

"If he's black, it probably is."

"He's not black," Nikki commented. "And he looks like he wants to come inside."

Sara set the costume on the table and got up to investigate. Just as Nikki said, there was a dog outside the door, but it wasn't Royal, her family's black Lab. It was a golden retriever who looked at her with the most woeful eyes she had ever seen on a dog. Even through the glass door she could hear the dog whimpering.

"He looks cold. Do you think he might be hurt?" Nikki asked.

"He's probably just looking for food." Her heart went out to the animal. Ever since she had been a child, she had collected strays. On more than one occasion her parents' home had been a temporary shelter while Sara found the animals a place to live.

The temptation to take this dog inside was great. It had been a long time since she had taken an abandoned animal under her wing. And she could see that this golden had been abandoned. He had that look about him. Unkempt. Lonesome. Uncollared.

"I'm not sure whose pet he is," she told Nikki.

"He looks really sad. He's shivering."

Sara couldn't resist. She opened the door. "All right. Come on in."

The dog limped past her into the Stable. "Oh, look! He's got a bad leg," Nikki said sympathetically.

It didn't take long for Sara to realize that the dog was a female "This is a girl dog, Nikki, and it looks to me like she's going to be a mom."

"Oh, no wonder she was crying. She doesn't have any place to have her babies."

"I'd better see what we can find to feed her." She led the dog into the kitchen where a half-eaten bagel sat on the counter.

"Do dogs like bagels?" Nikki asked.

"If they're hungry enough they do," Sara answered.

This golden was hungry enough. She scarfed it down in record time, then looked up at Sara for more. "I don't have anything else."

Nikki reached into her pocket. "I have some cookies Grandma gave me." She produced a plastic baggy with several iced sugar cookies inside.

The golden sniffed the bag appreciatively.

"She needs dog food." Sara reached for her coat and rummaged through the pockets until she found several crumpled dollar bills. "How would you like to run across the street to the Quick Stop and get her a can?"

"What kind?"

"Just ask Wally—he's the guy behind the counter—to find you something suitable for a golden." Nikki eagerly pulled on her cap and mittens, then headed out the door. "Oh, and if you have any money left over, buy yourself a candy bar."

While she was gone, Sara called her mother to ask if anyone in town had a pregnant golden with a limp. It was as she suspected. The dog didn't have a home.

By the time Nikki returned with the food, Sara had found a couple of old plastic bowls that she set on the floor in the back room. She poured water into one, then emptied the can of dog food into the other.

"What do you think her name is?" Nikki asked as she watched the golden eat.

Sara shrugged. "Maybe we should give her a new name. Do you have any suggestions?"

"I think we should call her Kris, as in Kris Kringle."

"Then Kris it is," Sara agreed.

"Would it be all right if I stayed here with her?" Nikki asked, obviously taken with the dog.

"Sure." Sara returned to her spot at the table, where she picked up the costume once more.

A few minutes later Nikki entered the bar, the golden trailing behind her. She hopped up onto one of the bar stools. Kris lay down beside her.

"I like this place," Nikki said, eyeing the silvery garland draped around the room. "This is the first bar I've ever been in. My dad said kids aren't supposed to go into the bars in California."

Sara smiled. "The Stable is really more of a restaurant...kind of a gathering place for the town."

"Grandma told me my dad used to work here."

"Yes, he did," Sara confirmed, her body warming at the mention of Joe.

"Did he wash the dishes?"

"I think mostly he swept the floors and helped Chester clean up at night after everyone left." Which was why he had the key to the place and how he and Sara were able to use it the night of prom.

"Were you and my dad friends?"

Friends? Somehow that description for her relationship with Joe didn't quite seem to fit. Although she had tried to be friends with him, it hadn't been easy. He had made it clear from the day he had arrived in town that he had wanted her to be his girl, flirting boldly with her, even when she was with her steady boyfriend.

She sidestepped Nikki's question, saying, "Everyone knows everyone else in a town this small."

"Grandma says everyone looks out for one another."

"Yes, they do."

"Then you must like it here."

"You're right. I do."

"I wish my dad did. He can't wait to go back home. He's not a cold-weather person," she explained.

Sara wanted to say Joe's dissatisfaction had little to do with the weather and a lot to do with the town itself, but she didn't. "Some people come to this part of the country just to play in the snow."

"I can see why. It's fun. Do you ice skate?" she asked.

"I used to when I was your age. There's a skating rink over at the park—or there used to be."

"Is that far from here?"

Sara smiled. "Nothing's far away in Christmas, Nikki. You can walk from one end of the town to the other. The park's just around the corner. You'll have to ask your dad to take you there."

"I've never skated outside before."

Sara glanced at Nikki's feet. "I might be able to find you a pair of skates to use. That is if you're going to be here long enough. How long are you staying in Christmas?"

"My dad wants to leave tomorrow, but I don't think we're going to."

"Why is that?"

She sighed. "My grandma doesn't want to go back to California with us."

"Did she tell your father she doesn't want to go?" Sara asked, feeling a tiny twinge of guilt at pumping the child for information.

Nikki nodded. "At dinner last night. Afterward they had a big argument that I wasn't supposed to hear, but I did. Grandma wants us to spend Christmas here with her."

Sara knew she should change the subject, but she couldn't resist asking, "Is there any reason why you can't?"

"We have to go over to Lindsey and Shawna's," Nikki answered. "They're my cousins. We go there every year. My uncle Charlie dresses up like Santa, and it's really fun."

"It's nice to be with family during the holidays, isn't it?" Sara commented.

"Mmm-hmm. I just wish we could be two places at once. Here with Grandma and with my cousins, too." She jumped down to go check on Kris, who had moved closer to the heating vent. "Are you going to take Kris home with you when you go?"

"First I'm going to take her to the vet and make sure she's okay."

As if the dog knew they were talking about her, she nuzzled her nose against Nikki's leg and groaned. Nikki reached down to scratch her under her chin.

"Will your mom let you keep Kris at home?" she asked.

"Oh, she'll probably fuss a little bit about it, but she's used to me bringing home stray animals. Do you have any pets?"

"We have a dog named Ralph."

"A little brown Chihuahua?"

She nodded. "How did you know?"

"Because your dad had Ralph when he was in high school." So he still had the dog he had taken with him when he left. Sara remembered how surprised she had been when she had first seen Joe's dog. Being that he was this tough city kid, she had expected he would be the owner of a big German shepherd or a husky, not a tiny little Chihuahua. "I bet you miss Ralph."

"Yeah, but it's been fun being at Grandma's," she said, her eyes lighting. "Her house is really neat and she lets me do all sorts of stuff my dad won't let me do. Last night we had a pillow fight and feathers got all over the floor and she didn't even care. She even moved my bed next to the window so I could see the stars."

"That sounds like something your grandmother would do. I hope you make a wish on the first one you see each night."

Nikki's eyes widened. "Do you wish upon the stars?"

"Every chance I get."

"Really?"

"Mmm-hmm. I started when I was about your age.

As soon as it was dark I'd say 'Star light, star bright...'"

"'First star I see tonight. Wish I may, wish I might, have my wish come true tonight,'" Nikki finished for her eagerly. "Then you believe that wishes come true?"

"Of course. Don't you?"

Nikki shrugged. "I guess they do."

Sara could see the skepticism in her eyes. "But you're not sure, are you?"

"I want to believe, but I've made so many wishes in the past that haven't come true...." She trailed off in uncertainty.

"You just have to be patient," Sara told her. "Sometimes it takes a lot of wishing on a lot of stars before you get any results."

Nikki nodded her head in understanding. Before Sara could ask her what kinds of things she wished for, Alice entered the Stable.

"Come on, Nik. We have to go feed your dad," she announced.

Nikki slipped her arms into her jacket. "Sara, if you're going to keep Kris at your house, do you think I could come see him?"

It was Alice who answered. "Maybe you could come with me when I go to have my costume fitted. Sara's making me a Mrs. Claus dress of red velvet. Wait until you see it, Nikki."

"You get to be Santa's wife?" Nikki's eyes grew round as saucers.

Alice nodded. "Aren't I lucky? Santa and I will be handing out candy at the North Pole."

"The North Pole? Where's that?"

"It's actually the old feed store next to the Quick Stop," her grandmother answered. "Kids will be able to get their picture taken with us. Of course I'll have to wear a wig because this hair of mine isn't the right color." She tugged on curls tinted an auburn brown, then she snapped her finger and turned to Sara. "You know what would be fun? If we could make Nikki an elf. Wouldn't that be adorable? She could be Santa's helper."

"Can I be an elf? Oh, please, please," Nikki begged, jumping up and down in excitement.

"Is there enough time to make her a costume?" Alice asked.

Sara paused in her stitching. "Actually we'd only need to make her shoe covers, a sash and a hat. She could wear a green turtleneck and leggings."

"And I could put red on my cheeks! And wear bells. Don't elves wear bells?" She wiggled around in anticipation. "Oh, it would be so much fun!"

Sara could see that Alice and Nikki were making plans without any regard for the fact that Joe intended to go back to California before the Victorian Christmas celebration ever began. Sara hated to be the one to burst their bubble, but she felt compelled to say something.

"Nikki, I think you would make a darling elf, but didn't you say you're spending Christmas in California?"

The animation disappeared from the young girl's face. "We are. I always sleep over at Lindsey and Shawna's."

Alice pulled her into her arms and gave her a hug. "Which is lots of fun. I know, I've been there. Santa comes with a sack full of presents and they play all sorts of games," she explained to Sara. Then she said to Nikki, "You don't want to play an elf in the cold when you can be with your cousins in that warm California sunshine.''

Sara wasn't so sure that Nikki agreed.

"Can I still see your costume?'' she asked her grandmother.

"Of course. And you can help me make the lining for my basket. I'm going to be giving out candy kisses.'' She looked at her watch. "Now we better get home and make your dad some lunch or he's going to get crabby.''

"He's been crabby ever since we got here,'' Nikki grumbled.

Sara was tempted to say "Don't I know it,'' but she bit her tongue. "How about if you stop by around four this afternoon for those alterations?'' She looked at Alice for confirmation.

"We'll be there. Maybe we can get Joe to come along. I'm sure you two would enjoy reminiscing,'' Alice said innocently.

Sara let the comment slide and was grateful when one of the city-council members came into the Stable and needed her attention. If there was one subject she didn't want to discuss, it was she and Joe ten years ago. And judging by the way he had behaved since his return, he was in no mood for nostalgia, either.

No, it would be best if she and Joe stayed as far away from each other as possible. There was no point in rekindling old memories or old feelings. Even if he could still make her heart beat a little faster just by looking at her.

Later that day

"DAD! LOOK WHAT Grandma found!'' Nikki raced into the living room clutching a copy of his high-school yearbook. She scrambled onto the sofa beside him and began leafing through the glossy pages.

"Where are you, Dad?" she asked, scanning the class photos.

He turned the page and placed a finger on his senior class photo. "Right there." His hair was long in the back and cut short on the top. He wore a bright yellow shirt with a skinny leather tie. Everyone else had sport coats. Not him. He had wanted to show all the kids in the small town that he marched to the beat of his own drum.

Nikki giggled. "You look funny."

"Styles change," he told her, remembering the tough-guy look he had put so much effort into achieving that day he had gone to have his picture taken.

"Where's Sara?" she wanted to know, peering closely at the other photos. Before he could put a finger on her picture, Nikki beat him to it saying, "There she is. She's got big hair."

Joe looked at the picture, remembering exactly how big that pouf of bangs had been. She had worn her hair permed, the long tresses falling in kinky waves down to her shoulders except for the clump of hair moussed to stand up like a cock's comb over her forehead.

As Nikki continued to turn the pages through the photos of various activities, he caught a glimpse of couples wearing fancy dresses and tuxedos. Prom night.

"Look, it's Sara. She's wearing a crown. Was she homecoming queen?"

"No, that's the prom king and queen."

"What's a prom?" Nikki asked.

"Just a dance," her father told her, his thoughts drifting back to that night over ten years ago. Sara had been at the formal dance with that geeky boyfriend of hers. Roger the Dodger. At least that's what Joe had nicknamed him because the guy had been afraid to fight and defend Sara's honor.

Joe had strutted into the school in his black jeans and a pink dress shirt, not caring that he had no date or that he hadn't bought a ticket. He had gone straight to the podium where the prom king and queen had just been crowned and motioned for Sara to come with him. He had nearly been thrown out by the principal, but then he had explained that he only needed to talk to Sara for a minute—that he had an urgent message to deliver to her.

Trusting that what he said was true, Sara had followed him into the school corridor, where he had swept her up into his arms and marched right out the door with her. He had dumped her into his cherry-red Camaro and driven away, laughing at how easy it had been.

He had planned to only drive around town for a few minutes and let her know exactly what he thought about her plan to save the prom from extinction, but then something had happened. She hadn't been angry at him for crashing the dance and taking her away. She had asked him why he hated the prom and he had told her. She had listened to him criticize nearly every aspect of their high-school life with something he hadn't expected. Understanding. She'd made him feel as if what he thought was important.

Then he had taken her back to the Stable, where he had challenged her to prove to him that she wasn't the Goody Two-shoes everyone said she was. Never would he have expected that she'd accept the challenge. But she had, getting a little drunk, welcoming him into her arms as they danced intimately and then falling asleep in his arms after he had touched her in places she had never allowed even Roger the Dodger to touch her.

"Those pictures must be stirring fond memories," he heard his mother say. "You're sitting there with a rather sly smile on your face."

He realized then that he had been daydreaming. About Sara. And just as it had ten years ago, his body had reacted to the sensual thoughts in a typically male way. He shifted uncomfortably on the couch.

"Actually I was thinking about money," he lied, avoiding his mother's suspicious glare.

"Dad, what does 's.w.a.k.' mean?" Nikki asked, having found the autograph section of the yearbook.

He took the book out of her hands as he remembered that not all of the messages were suitable for a nine-year-old's eyes. "Sealed with a kiss."

She giggled. "Did your girlfriend write that?"

He tweaked a curl on her head and grinned. "One of them did."

"Your father had lots of girlfriends, Nikki. He was the best-looking boy in town, and all the girls wanted to go out with him," his mother stated proudly, which only produced another round of giggles from his daughter.

"What about Sara? Was she one of your girlfriends, too?" Nikki asked, still smiling.

He avoided answering her question by saying, "Your grandma's pulling your leg. I didn't have any girlfriends in town."

Nikki was still looking at the yearbook. "Didn't you really have any girlfriends here, Dad?"

"Nope. There's only been one girl in my life. Your mother."

Which wasn't entirely true. For just one night Sara had been his girl. And at the time he had thought it would last longer than one night. But it hadn't. Because although he had thought Sara was different from the rest of the kids in town, he had discovered that she was just like everyone else. Small town.

That's why he had left right after graduation and never looked back. If there was one thing he had learned at an early age, it was not to long for something that was unattainable. And that's what Sara was. She had her heart set on being another man's girl.

Obviously it hadn't been all she had hoped it would be. Now she was back in Christmas alone. No husband. No moussed-up bangs. Just Sara, plain and pretty.

And he was getting aroused just thinking about her.

THAT NIGHT as Nikki lay in bed looking out her window, she was disappointed to see no stars. The only bright light came from the star atop the water tower, which she decided she might have to use to make her wish if it continued to be cloudy in Christmas.

The absence of stars didn't keep her from talking to her mother, however. It had been an exciting day, one she needed to share.

"I think it might be time for me to make that wish, Mom. There's this lady named Sara and she's nice. She's doing all sorts of nice things for the people here and she smiles a lot and she takes in stray animals. And she's pretty, too. The best part is that she believes in wishing on the stars, too. She even knew the same rhyme that you taught me."

She closed her eyes and thought about the conversation she had had with Sara that morning. "There's only one small problem, Mom. She doesn't like Dad. Could you ask God to let the stars come out? I'm going to need some help with this one."

Chapter Five

December 18, 7:00 p.m.

"Joe, get your coat on. The sleigh is here."

"What does a sleigh have to do with me?" he asked as his mother stood with his jacket in her hands, holding it out so that he could slip his arms inside.

"Buzz is going to be giving sleigh rides at the Victorian Christmas celebration. I want you to take a test ride tonight. Come," she insisted, giving his jacket a little shake to encourage him to hurry.

He stared at her in disbelief. "You're joking, right?"

"No, I'm not joking. Nikki's expecting you to pick her up—she's with Auntie Jean—and Buzz is going to take you there in the sleigh so we can make sure the ride's a smooth one."

"Wouldn't someone else be a better judge of that? Like someone who lives here and likes to ride around outside in the cold?"

"You don't want to disappoint Nikki, do you?"

She knew just which button to push. He groaned and put on his jacket.

"It'll be fun," his mother said.

Obviously his idea of fun and his mother's were not

the same. "I wish you would have asked me about this before you went ahead and arranged it."

"It was kind of a last-minute thing." She dismissed his complaint with a nonchalance that had him looking at her rather suspiciously. She handed him his gloves, a plaid blanket and a thermos.

"What's this for?" he asked, holding up the insulated bottle.

"Hot chocolate. To keep you warm. Now quit frowning and make this fun for your daughter," she scolded lightly and shoved him out the door.

"Hey, Joe! I hear you get to be the guinea pig." Buzz Gustafson greeted him with a wave of a gloved hand.

"So my mother tells me. It looks like you've been busy," he said, noticing the fresh coat of paint as he stepped up into the sleigh.

"She's been in the barn for the past fifteen years," the older man said from his position up front in the driver's seat. "Never had any reason to use it after the kids all left home. You comfortable back there?" he asked as Joe settled himself onto the worn leather seat.

"Sure. I'm fine. I'm ready whenever you are."

"We're lucky the streets are snow packed," he said as the horses pulled the sleigh away from the curb. "The runners are a little rusty. How's she riding?"

"Just fine," Joe answered.

"That's good. Of course, the real test will be when we pick up Sara."

The mention of the woman's name woke up his hormones. "You're picking up Sara?"

Buzz didn't answer but turned the corner, stopping in front of the Richards' home. Joe could see Sara standing inside, gazing out the front window, a red cap perched on her blond curls. As soon as she saw the sleigh, she tugged on a pair of red mittens and came outside.

"Hey there, Sara. You ready for your ride?" Buzz called out to her. "It's a perfect night. No wind, lots of stars."

Joe noticed that she looked up at the sky as she came down the front walk. "You're right, Buzz. It's a great night for a sleigh ride." When she noticed Joe sitting in the sleigh, she hesitated briefly.

"Watch your step getting inside," Buzz warned her as she neared the sleigh.

Joe jumped up to give Sara a hand. Reluctantly she took it, whispering, "What are you doing here?"

"Maybe I should ask you the same thing," he answered, allowing her to get comfortable before he sat back down.

"My mother asked me to do a trial run in this thing before we use it for the Victorian Christmas celebration," she explained, sliding as far away from him as possible in the narrow confines of the sleigh.

"Well, now that's interesting because that's the same thing my mother said to me." They both looked toward the house and saw Eugenia Richards peeking out behind a curtain. Sara closed her eyes and shook her head, mumbling, "Good grief."

"You two ready back there?" Buzz called back to them.

They both eyed each other suspiciously before saying ready in unison.

Neither one said another word as the sleigh glided across the snow-covered streets. A few moments of silence stretched into an uncomfortable few minutes. When the sleigh left the road and traveled onto a farmer's field, Joe asked Buzz, "Where are we going?"

"To pick up your daughter," the driver replied.

"Jean lives over on Third Street," Joe reminded him.

"She ain't at Jean's. She's at Martha's."

"She and Jean went over to the farm to see Martha's homemade gingerbread house," Sara explained.

"Which is the reason for this," Joe said, holding up the thermos. Seeing Sara's puzzled look, he added, "My mom filled it with hot chocolate and sent it along."

"That was sweet of her," Sara remarked.

"Wasn't it?" he drawled sarcastically, knowing that his mother had deliberately arranged for him and Sara to be alone on the sleigh.

Another silence stretched between them. Joe wanted to start a conversation, but every time he had seen Sara in the past few days she'd been hostile toward him. So he used the hot chocolate as an olive branch. "Would you like some?" He held up the thermos.

"Sure, thanks." He passed her the thermos, then watched as she poured a small amount into the cap. She took a sip, then licked her lips. It wasn't meant to be a sensual gesture, but that's exactly how Joe saw it. He knew that were he to kiss that mouth, it would be all warm and chocolate tasting. Desire stirred inside him.

"You folks having a good time?" Buzz asked over his shoulder.

"It's lovely, Buzz." Sara turned to Joe and said, "Isn't this fun, Joe?"

He wanted to disagree, but the truth was he did enjoy gliding over the snow beneath a carpet of stars with Sara beside him. "You're doing a good job, Buzz. The sleigh's going to be just fine."

"It's not too rough of a ride?" Buzz wanted to know.

"Not at all," Joe answered. "Actually it's quite smooth."

"It helps to have a pretty girl sitting alongside you," Buzz said on a chuckle.

Joe met Sara's eyes. "Yes, it does."

She focused her attention on the hot chocolate, pretending she hadn't heard him. He slid closer to her and said, "You are still just as pretty as you were back in high school, Sara."

She ignored his compliment. "I was thinking...maybe we should provide hot chocolate on the sleigh ride. Jean is going to be serving it at Mother Goose Land. We could have the sleigh depart from there."

He leaned ever closer and said in a voice meant only for her ears, "You never did like me paying you compliments, did you?"

She slid closer to the side wall. "They were more than compliments, Joe. They were passes, and in case you've forgotten, I was going steady with Roger."

"What about now? Are you going steady with anyone?"

There was another silence. She wasn't going to answer him. She was giving him the brush-off, just as she had done in high school. Maybe that's why he was still attracted to her—because she acted as if she wasn't interested in him.

"Sara?"

"No, there is no one," she said quietly.

He was glad there was no one and was about to tell her he was when Buzz turned around and said, "Looks like someone's waiting for us!" They weren't far from a big white farmhouse that had a mercury-vapor lamp lighting the area around it.

Joe looked up to see Nikki running toward the sleigh, waving her arms excitedly. As soon as the sleigh came to a stop, she hopped up inside and plunked herself down smack dab in the middle of Joe and Sara.

"I've never been on a sleigh ride. Isn't this awesome, Dad?"

"Awesome," Joe repeated, wishing that Sara were the one who would have been sitting in the middle and that the hand clutching his arm belonged to her, not his daughter.

December 19, 4:30 p.m.

"DAD, AREN'T YOU COMING?" Nikki stood bundled up in her snowsuit and mittens, waiting for her father, who sat at the kitchen table, his fingers punching keys on his laptop.

"Can't, Nik, I have work to do," he answered, feeling a bit frustrated that he was sitting at his laptop in Minnesota rather than in his office in California.

"But what are you gonna eat for dinner?"

"I'm sure your grandma has food in the refrigerator," he said, his eyes on the numbers popping up on the screen.

Nikki moaned in disappointment. "But I want you to come."

"I can't. I told you, I have work to do."

She refused to take no for an answer. "But don't you want to see the tree and hear the Christmas carols? And see Grandma be Mrs. Claus?"

That caught his attention. "Grandma is going to be what?"

As if on cue, his mother entered the kitchen wearing a red velvet robe with white cuffs and collar.

She sashayed in front of them and asked, "Well, how do I look?"

"It's perfect, Grandma," Nikki gushed affectionately. "I like your hat."

"Sara did a beautiful job, don't you think?" she asked Joe.

"Sara made that?"

"Mmm-hmm. She's a wonderful seamstress. She's making Nikki an elf costume, but it's not quite finished."

"It's green with pointy toes and a hat—" Nikki began, only to have her father interrupt her.

"Why do you need an elf costume?" he asked, his brows furrowing.

"For the Victorian Christmas celebration." It was his mother who answered. "I'm going to be Mrs. Claus, Sam Hanson is going to be Santa and Nikki will be an elf passing out candy to the kids." Seeing the look on Joe's face, she quickly added, "We thought we'd make her the costume just in case you're still here on Christmas Eve."

Before Joe could tell her that it wasn't even a possibility, his mother added, "Why are you still working? Aren't you coming along to the tree lighting?"

"I'd rather stay here and work," he answered flatly.

"Tell Dad he has to go," Nikki begged her grandmother. "You're his mother. He'll listen to you."

That caused Alice to laugh. "Your father hasn't listened to me in a long time, dear." Then she turned to Joe and said, "You hate cooking for yourself. Are you sure you don't want to come with us?"

He wrinkled his nose. "To eat hot-dish and Jell-O? I'll pass on that particular gourmet feast."

Alice give Nikki a gentle shove toward the door.

"Why don't you go out on the front step and watch for Auntie Jean. I need to get some bobby pins for my hat to make sure it doesn't fall off."

Nikki nodded and zipped out the door. As soon as she was gone, his mother let him have it. "Just because you don't want anything to do with the people of Christmas doesn't mean you have a right to spoil your daughter's fun."

"And what fun would that be? Standing in the freezing cold and watching the lights come on a tree while off-key voices sing 'Joy to the World'?" he drawled sarcastically.

His mother shoved her hands on her waist. "If you didn't want to celebrate the holidays, Joe, why did you come home?"

"To check up on my mother, who I thought was convalescing from a broken foot."

"Look." She lifted her skirt and stuck out her foot that no longer had the walking cast. "It's fine."

"Was it ever broken? Or were the crutches for effect?"

She raised her hand in an threatening manner, as if to strike him. "You know what would have happened if you had used that tone with me when you were a boy."

He dropped the sarcasm. "I'm sorry, Mom. I came became I was worried about you."

"And as I told you on the phone, I'm a grown woman, Joseph. I can take care of myself."

He knew whenever she called him Joseph she was running out of patience. He rubbed a hand across the back of his neck where muscles kinked. "All right, Mom. You've made your point."

"Oh, but I haven't. You didn't just come here to

check up on me. You came because you thought you could get me to go back to California with you. When I told you I wasn't coming out for the holidays, you decided to use the only weapon you have to get your way." She paused, then added in a low voice, "Nikki."

"She wanted to see her grandmother."

"And you always try to give her what she wants."

"When it comes to family, I do. Ever since Angela, died I've done everything I can to make sure she is surrounded by family as much as possible, which is why it's so important you're with her at Christmas. That's why I came here. To try to make you understand that Nikki needs you around the holidays...just as she needs Angela's mother, her cousins and aunts and uncles."

Alice took the chair next to his and placed her hand on his forearm. "I don't want to spend this Christmas in California, Joe. I've explained to Nikki why I don't and I believe she understands. You, apparently, don't."

He could feel his patience slipping away. "What I don't understand is this attitude you have that helping a dying town raise money is more important than being with your granddaughter."

"I'm needed here, Joe."

He sighed. "Mom, how many times do I have to tell you this little campaign Sara Richards has cooked up isn't going to save the town? And if you think your being here is going to make a difference to the outcome...well, I hate to tell you this, but you're wrong."

This time she was the one who sighed. "The reason I'm staying to help out is because this town has become my family, Joe. We're in a crisis and I wouldn't feel right leaving them. I don't *want* to leave them, so please don't ask me to."

Joe leaned back in his chair and studied her silently

for a moment before saying, "You're determined to stay, aren't you?"

Nikki poked her head back inside the door. "Grandma, Auntie Jean's waiting for us at the corner."

"I'll be right there, sweetie," she told her granddaughter, who dashed out just as quickly as she dashed in. To Joe she said, "I understand if you and Nikki must go back, but this year I'm spending Christmas here. Now I suggest you make the most of the time we have together and come with us to the tree-lighting ceremony and the potluck supper."

It was her maternal voice of authority, the one that always put him on the defensive. "I think it's better if I stay home by myself tonight."

"How can you say that after spouting all that stuff about wanting to surround Nikki with family at this time of the year?" She lifted the heavy velvet robe as she stood. "Maybe you better start practicing what you're preaching, Joe."

"Ma, I don't need to be lectured." He hated the fact that she could make him feel like a kid who needed a reprimand.

She pulled her coat on over the red velvet dress. "This is a special night for Nikki. Do you really want to miss it?" And with those parting words she walked out the door.

If it had been her intention to make him feel like Scrooge, she had succeeded. He got up to look out the kitchen window. The sun had just set, leaving a twilight that made the snow glisten on the lawns and rooftops. He could see Nikki walking between her grandmother and Auntie Jean, her legs hopping and skipping as they walked toward the park.

He sighed and rubbed a hand across his jaw. Going

to the tree-lighting ceremony meant he'd see many of the people who had made him feel like an outsider when he had lived in the small town. And of course Sara would be there. Bossing everybody around. Arguing with him every chance she had. Tempting him with that smile that could make every hormone in his body hyperactive.

Just thinking about her caused his body to react in a purely physical way. Geesh, he must be in a sorry state if he could get excited about a woman who had ripped his heart out and stamped on it with her small-town attitude. The sooner he left Christmas the better.

But first he would go to find his daughter and watch the lighting of the tree in the town square. And eat the potluck supper. And put up with the curious looks he knew would come his way from all those folks who hadn't wanted him in Christmas the last time he had been here. And watch Sara try to rally the town together.

Because in two days he would be gone.

"THERE ARE 272 LIGHTS on this tree," Sara announced to the crowd gathered around the tall pine in Daniel Griffin park. "One for every resident of Christmas."

A round of applause and whistles punctuated her words.

"As you all know, money's been tight this year, but when we asked everyone to contribute one dollar so that we could light this tree, there wasn't a single person in Christmas who didn't chip in to make this possible." More applause filled the air.

"This tree isn't just a decoration for our holiday celebration. It's an example of what we can do as a community. It represents the spirit of a town that won't allow anyone to force us out of business.''

Again she was interrupted by applause.

"Each bulb on this tree represents the hope we have in the future. We will not let the lights go out in our town.'' Another round of applause had her pausing.

"At this time I'd like to ask Nikki Gibson to come up here,'' Sara announced to the small crowd.

With a bit of bewilderment on her face, Nikki climbed the steps of the temporary platform. When she reached the top, Sara put her arms on her shoulders and turned her around to face the crowd.

"As most of you know, Nikki is here visiting her grandmother, Alice Gibson. She wanted to do something special for the tree of lights, so she collected pop cans and turned them into the recycling center. The cash she received she then gave to the Saving Christmas committee so that we could buy a star for the top of the tree.''

At the sound of applause Nikki beamed proudly.

"That's why the Saving Christmas committee decided to let Nikki be the one who turns on the lights.'' Sara reached for the power strip and set it in front of the little girl.

"I get to light the tree?'' she asked, excitement dancing in her eyes.

"Yes. All you have to do is press that red button.''

Nikki removed her mitten, licked her lips, then placed her finger on the power switch. Instantly hundreds of colored lights glowed on the branches of the tall pine. She grinned, the crowd cheered and Sara couldn't remember the last time she had had such a warm feeling inside her.

Next several students stepped up onto the platform to

lead the crowd in a rendition of "O Christmas Tree." When they had finished, it was time for the tuba band to take the stage. In a town the size of Christmas, Sara could hardly believe they had ten tuba players who practiced regularly and gave concerts twice a year.

While they entertained the crowd with Christmas music, Alice Gibson motioned to Sara that she was heading over to the church to prepare for the potluck supper. Sara offered to bring Nikki with her as soon as the program was finished.

A short while later, Sara made the announcement that dinner would be served in the church basement. She was about to take Nikki by the hand when Joe appeared.

"Dad! You're here!" Nikki threw her arms around his waist in a bear hug. "Did you see me turn on the lights?"

"Yes, I saw you. I was in the back."

"And did you see my star on top of the tree?" She aimed her finger skyward.

"It's a beautiful star, Nikki. You did a good job." He gave her another squeeze.

"I'm glad you're here, Dad. Now you can come to the potluck supper. Grandma's serving food, so I'm going to sit with Sara. She's going to walk me over to the church so I don't get lost 'cause Grandma already left."

Joe looked at Sara and said, "Thank you for taking care of Nikki, but now that I'm here, I can see that she gets to eat dinner."

It was a dismissal. Sara thought he might as well have told her to get lost. Annoyed, she said, "I'm surprised you are here. Your mother said you weren't coming."

"I wouldn't miss my daughter lighting this beautiful tree," he said, causing Nikki's grin to expand.

· "We can still eat with Sara, can't we, Dad?" Nikki wanted to know.

Joe's eyes met Sara's. She could see that he didn't want to have dinner with her. It was there in his face, yet she could also see that he was reluctant to disappoint his daughter.

"Sara probably has official duties to perform," he answered, obviously looking for a way out. "Being that she's the chairperson of the Saving Christmas committee, that is."

Nikki may not have noticed the undercurrent of tension in the air, but Sara did. It would have been easy to take the excuse he offered. All she had to do was tell Nikki she probably should make sure everything was running smoothly at the dinner. But that was exactly what Joe wanted her to do.

And the last thing she wanted to do was let him have his way. Not after the way he'd been treating her since he'd been back. No, she wanted to make Joe Gibson uncomfortable. Just as uncomfortable as his presence in town was making her feel. So she said with an artificial smile, "No, no more duties for me."

The three of them walked the short distance to the church, with Nikki chattering cheerfully. Once inside, they headed for the basement, where they hung their jackets in the coatroom and then made their way into the food hall.

"There's a lot of people here," Nikki commented as they took their places in the buffet line.

"This is a happy time of the year, and everyone's feeling positive about our campaign to save Christmas," Sara told her. She could see by the skepticism on Joe's face that he was the only one who wasn't thinking along those lines.

"Look! There's Grandma with Santa." Nikki's attention was drawn to the couple circling the room greeting people.

Sara saw Joe's eyes narrow as he looked at his mother with Sam Hanson.

"Remember Mr. Hanson from English class?" Sara asked. "Why are you frowning? Wasn't he one of your favorites?"

"I'm not frowning," he denied.

While they stood in line, the same six students who had led the caroling at the park provided background music during dinner. Sara didn't need to worry about making small talk with Joe. Nikki chatted nonstop about all the differences she had discovered between the small town of Christmas and the city where they lived.

Many of the people they passed said hello to her, which had Joe asking, "You've met quite a few people since we've been here, haven't you?"

"Everyone's working on the campaign, Dad, and when they find out who I am they all stop to tell me stories about you when you were a teenager."

"What do they say about me?"

She shrugged. "Mostly what a nice boy you were."

Joe chuckled. "That's a first."

Sara sent him a warning glance, which he answered with a lift of his brows.

"Were you a hottie, Dad?"

"A hottie?" he asked.

"You know, a guy all the girls want to date?"

Joe looked at Sara and said, "Maybe you should ask Sara that question."

The look he gave her was enough to make her breath catch in her throat. Ten years ago she would have looked away, embarrassed. Not today.

"Was he a hottie, Sara?" Nikki wanted to know.

"Yes, he was." She answered Nikki, but her eyes were held by Joe's. "All the girls thought he was so cute and they all would have loved to have been his girl."

Nikki made a sound of disbelief. "Really?"

"And why is that so hard to believe?" Joe asked, folding his arms across his chest. "I was the best-dressed guy in the senior class. Even ask Sara."

Nikki looked to her for confirmation. "He was. He'd come walking down the hall at school, and girls would swoon over him," she said with a teasing grin.

"But not Sara," Joe stated, holding her gaze in an almost challenging way.

No, but the way he looked tonight, dressed in a sweater and casual slacks, she could have easily swooned over him now. Ten years may have passed but he still had the power to make her go a little weak in the knees, though it wasn't something she wanted Nikki to know about.

"I had a steady boyfriend long before your dad ever moved to town," Sara told the little girl, and noticed that the flirtatious twinkle in Joe's eyes disappeared.

They had reached the food table, putting an end to their conversation as Nikki went on one side and her father on the other. Sara followed Nikki, answering her questions as to what some of the unknown dishes contained.

When their plates were full, they found three spots at the same table where Sara's parents sat. Sara felt as if she were under a magnifying glass, for she could see her mother eyeing Joe curiously. Lots of curious glances came their way, and Sara was certain that it wasn't only her mother who was wondering just what—if any-thing—was going on between the two of them.

It didn't help that Joe flirted shamelessly with her, much to Nikki's delight. At least he did until he noticed that his mother was awfully chummy with Santa. Sara had never seen Alice's face so animated and realized that the rumors she had heard regarding Sam and Alice being more than friends could very well be true.

When Mr. and Mrs. Claus passed out sweets to their table, Alice paused in front of Joe to say, "You remember Sam Hanson, don't you, Joe?"

Joe stood to shake the man's hand. "We talked at the hardware store the other day."

"I think you make a perfect Mr. and Mrs. Claus," Sara's mother remarked, which Sara noticed brought a frown to Joe's face.

"This is our trial run for the Victorian Christmas celebration. We're honing up on our ho-ho-ho's," Alice remarked.

"We're going to be spreading good cheer, listening to wishes, putting people in a holiday mood...that sort of thing," Sam added.

"Sounds as if you have your work cut out for you," Eugenia commented.

"It's not easy being the Clauses. What we really could use is an elf," Santa said with a twinkle in his eye. "Maybe I'll get one for Christmas." He looked expectantly at Sara.

"I'm sewing as fast as I can," she told him.

"And doing a beautiful job," Alice complimented, then turned to Sam. "Come, we better move along." She looped her arm through his and gently nudged him. As he passed Nikki he tweaked her braid.

Nikki giggled and said to her father, "Aren't they cute? Grandma looks really happy, doesn't she?"

Sara noticed how closely Joe watched the pair move away with arms locked, Alice's cheeks flushed by something Sam had whispered in her ear.

"Is it true Nikki's going to be an elf?" Eugenia asked Joe, whose brow furrowed at the question.

"We're not going to be here on Christmas Eve, Mrs. Richards," he replied.

"Oh, that's too bad. I know your mother would love to have you stay," she crooned sympathetically.

"So when are you leaving, Joe?" Sara asked.

"Tomorrow morning."

Nikki made a sound of protest. "You didn't tell me we were leaving tomorrow."

"We were supposed to leave yesterday, but you wanted to stay for the tree lighting so I changed our flight," he reminded her.

"But Sara's not done with my elf costume." Distress choked her words.

"It's all right, Nikki. I can finish it tonight and drop it off first thing in the morning," Sara tried to reassure her.

"You'd do that?" Nikki asked, wide-eyed.

Sara nodded and the little girl beamed.

She leaned over and wrapped her arms around Sara's waist. "Thank you. You're so sweet." Then she turned to Joe and said, "Isn't Sara sweet, Dad?"

"Yes, she's sweet," Joe agreed, and the look in his eyes sent more than a tingle through Sara's body. It practically had every nerve in her body singing. It was the same look that had been there when they had been on the sleigh ride and he had told her she was pretty.

She quickly lowered her eyes and fumbled with her

fork, scooping up a taste of the pumpkin pie before her. It was a good thing he was leaving tomorrow. This time there was no Roger to stop her from doing something she might regret.

Suddenly whistles and laughter filled the room. All heads turned toward the arched entryway of the dining hall. Standing beneath a sprig of mistletoe were Alice and Sam, arms locked about each other as they kissed.

"Way to go, Santa," someone called out.

Sara noticed Joe wasn't smiling.

"Can I go get another glass of cider?" Nikki asked him, but he paid no attention.

It was Eugenia who pushed back her chair and said, "Come with me, Nikki. I'll get you some."

Sara's father also rose to his feet to go visit a friend. That left Joe and Sara alone. She wanted to escape with the others, but Joe stopped her.

"I need to ask you something."

Sara's heart skipped a beat. "Ask away," she said, expecting it had something to do with the two of them. It didn't.

"What's going on between my mother and Sam Hanson?" he asked.

Sara feigned ignorance. "How would I know?"

"Because you live here and everyone in Christmas knows everything about everyone else." It was said without any malice, but Sara didn't care. She took it as a criticism.

She shoved her chair back and gathered up her things. "Why must you constantly put down everyone in this town? If you want to know what's happening with your mother, ask her." She picked up her plate and started to walk away just as Nikki and her mother were returning.

"Where are you going, Sara?" the little girl asked.

"I think I'd better see if they need any help with cleanup in the kitchen," Sara answered, trying not to look at Joe.

"Can I help?" she asked.

Before Sara could answer, Joe spoke up. "Nikki, we'd better go back to Grandma's. You need to pack your things."

"But it's my last night in Christmas," she pleaded.

Sara saw Joe's face soften. "I know. How about if I let you stay for another half hour and then come back and pick you up? Would that help?"

She nodded vigorously.

"You go help Sara and I'll tell Grandma, okay?" Joe said in a voice Sara hadn't heard in a long time. It was full of tenderness and love. Then he turned to Sara and said, "I'll pick her up out front in half an hour."

Sara led Nikki to the kitchen, where they donned aprons. As they worked together clearing dishes from the tables, she couldn't stop thinking about Joe. The look that had been in his eyes when he had said she was sweet. The flirtatious grins he had cast her way.

Unable to resist, Sara asked Nikki about her father as they cleaned. She didn't want to be curious about their life in California, but she was, and Nikki was delighted to tell her about it.

"Sounds like you'll have a fun time on Christmas," she commented when the little girl had explained their holiday plans.

"Uh-huh," she said reaching for a plastic fork that had fallen on the floor.

They worked side by side and before Sara knew it, the half hour had flown by. As she untied Nikki's apron from around her waist, the young girl asked, "Do you believe in miracles, Sara?"

"Yes, I do."

"Me, too." Before Sara could ask her what miracle she was hoping would occur, she saw her father coming toward her. "My dad's here. I gotta go."

With a wave goodbye, she skipped away. She wasn't gone but ten minutes when Sara noticed the red ribbon that had been tied to Nikki's braid was lying on the floor. She looked around the room for Alice, hoping to give it to her, but the older woman was nowhere in sight.

With a sigh Sara stuffed the ribbon in her pocket. A short while later as she headed for home, she decided to drop it off at the Gibson house. As she approached the brightly lit yard, she heard a voice.

It belonged to Nikki. She sat on a bench in Alice's backyard talking. It was only as Sara drew nearer that she realized that the nine-year-old was alone, her head tipped back as she stared up at the sky.

"I hope you can hear me, Mom. The stars aren't out tonight, but I think I see one little bitty star so I hope the window to heaven is open."

Sara swallowed back a lump in her throat.

"I need your help really bad," Nikki continued speaking out loud. "Mrs. Bergstrom says miracles can happen if you're patient, and I've been really patient, Mom—you know that."

Sara knew she should announce her presence, but something stopped her. Maybe it was the way Nikki looked sitting on the bench. Shoulders slumped, trying hard not to give in to the temptation to cry.

The little girl thought she was alone, which was why

Sara didn't make her presence known. She didn't want to ruin that sense of tranquillity she heard in her voice.

She carefully began to back away and pretend that she hadn't overhead Nikki's soliloquy. Before she was out of hearing range, she heard Nikki say, "Please make dad understand why I want to stay at Grandma's for Christmas. For the first time since you've been gone, I don't feel lonely at Christmas. I found a place where everyone is nice to me. This town is nice and Grandma is really cool. Please, Mom, you have to give Dad a sign that we should stay."

Sara stood frozen to the spot, a lump in her throat. Suddenly she knew what she had to do. Without saying a word to Nikki, she went around to the front of the house, where she rang the bell.

Within a few seconds Joe answered. He looked just as attractive as he had earlier that evening. He still wore the oatmeal-colored sweater and the dark green corduroys.

"Sara. This is a surprise." He gestured for her to step inside.

She stomped the snow from her boots and stepped onto the scatter rug inside the door. "I came to return this." She handed him the red ribbon. "Nikki left it at the church."

"Thank you. I'll give it to her when she comes in. She's out back playing in the snow."

"I know. I saw her when I came around the corner."

He looked perplexed. "Then why didn't you just give her the ribbon?"

Sara wasn't sure what she should say to Joe. All she knew was that something had to be said. "Nikki was having a private conversation I didn't want to interrupt."

His brows drew together. "A conversation? I thought she was alone."

"She is."

"She's talking to herself?"

"Not exactly."

When Joe continued to stare at her in bewilderment she said, "She's talking to her mother."

He stiffened.

"I only heard a couple of sentences, but it was obvious that she wants to spend Christmas here with her grandmother," Sara answered.

He folded his arms in front of his chest. "Is that why you really came over here? To try to convince me to let my daughter stay for your celebration?"

"No, I told you I came to return the ribbon. I just happened to overhear Nikki talking to her mother and I thought you'd want to know what she said." She could see by the look on his face that he didn't believe her.

"If Nikki wants to stay in Christmas, why hasn't she told me?"

"Maybe she's afraid to."

"Afraid?" He chuckled in disbelief. "My daughter is not afraid of me."

"Maybe she doesn't want to disappoint you. If she thinks it's important to you that you go back to California, she might not be telling you what she really wants because she doesn't want to spoil your Christmas."

He stood there staring at her, slowly shaking his head. "My daughter doesn't need you to come to her rescue, Sara. She's not in any danger nor is she a victim of a big bad daddy."

He was laughing at her, as if she were embellishing

what she had heard outside. "Nikki *was* talking to her mother," she stated in no uncertain terms.

"I don't doubt that for a minute."

"But you don't believe me when I say that she was asking her mother to help her find a way to let her stay here for Christmas." He didn't deny her statement. "I'm not a liar, Joe. Why won't you believe me?"

"You mean the way I believed you ten years ago when you told me that you were going to break up with Roger because you loved me?"

She knew she had hurt him badly back then, but she hadn't expected he'd still carry it with him. "It wouldn't have worked out between us, Joe," she said softly.

"Not as long as we were here in this town," he said derisively.

"It had nothing to do with the town!"

"It had everything to do with this town, Sara," he argued. "I was an outsider. There was nothing I could have done or said that would have made me good enough to date the most popular girl in school."

"I already had a boyfriend." She ran her fingers through her hair in frustration. "Oh, why are we arguing about this now? This has nothing to do with Nikki."

"Oh, that's right. You came because of your concern for Nikki," he tossed back at her snidely.

"Yes, I did, but I can see I could have saved myself the trip." She reached for the doorknob. "You can blame me and the town all you want, Joe, for what happened ten years ago, but the truth is you didn't want to belong here. And because you didn't like the town, I wasn't supposed to like it, either. Did you ever think that maybe the problem was we were just too young to know better?" And without another word she left.

All the way home Sara thought about Joe. Ten years ago he had wanted her to leave town with him, to give up the life she knew and move to California. When she had refused, he had left without her and never looked back.

He still had those bad feelings about the town. And now they were causing him to deprive his daughter of spending Christmas with her grandmother. The more Sara thought about it, the more she was bothered by the injustice of it all.

Nikki loved being with her grandmother, and Alice Gibson was devoted to her granddaughter. On many occasions she had told Sara how much she wished Joe would allow Nikki to stay for the holidays.

If only there was a way Sara could make it happen.

Suddenly she realized there was a way to make it happen. She could put a kink in his plans. If he were to miss his plane, he and Nikki would have to stay in Christmas. Nikki would be able to be an elf for the Victorian Christmas celebration. Alice would have her granddaughter with her for the holidays. And Sara would have the satisfaction of knowing that she had made two people's lives happier.

Was it such a preposterous idea? Sara didn't think so. After all, look what Joe had prevented her from doing ten years ago. She had missed being the queen of the prom because he had wanted his way. What if he missed going home for Christmas?

The more Sara thought about it, the more she liked the idea. Not only would it give Nikki what she wanted, but Sara could also show Joe that he was all wrong about her. She didn't champion hopeless causes and she could succeed if she wanted to.

She'd show him. Tomorrow.

Chapter Six

December 20, 9:30 a.m.

"Mom, where's Nikki?" Joe asked the following morning when the last of the suitcases had been loaded into the car.

"Jean took her over to Sara's to pick up her elf costume," Alice replied.

He glanced at his watch. "You did tell her to come straight home, didn't you? We need to leave by ten if we're going to get to the airport on time."

"I'm sure she'll be here, dear."

Just then the phone rang. Joe could only hear his mother's end of the conversation.

"Uh-huh. Okay. Are you sure? Okay. Fifteen minutes, right? Okay. Bye, sweetie." She hung up the phone and turned to Joe. "That was Nikki. She's going over to the Mother Goose Land to get a book that Jean promised her. She wants you to pick her up there."

"Then I might as well leave now and get her on my way out of town," Joe suggested, which produced a frown on his mother's face.

"Oh, you can't do that. Nikki and I haven't said our goodbyes," she fretted. "Why don't you walk over to the Stable and get her? That way I can finish loading your things in the car. I want to give you some treats to take with you for the long drive to the airport.''

Joe sighed. Just what he didn't want to do was put his boots back on and trudge through the snow another time. "I'd rather drive."

She clicked her tongue. "The walk will do you good. You're going to be cramped up all day in the car and on the plane.''

He knew she had a point.

With a grimace he tugged on the Sorels, reached for his jacket and headed out the door. Instead of putting a stocking hat on his head, he wore his Dodgers baseball cap. As he walked toward Main Street, he turned up the collar on his suede jacket and ducked his head to avoid the sting of the wind. A horn caused him to glance sideways.

"Hey, Joe. Can I give you a lift?"

Sitting behind the wheel of a station wagon was Sara. A very jaunty-looking Sara. Blond curls dangled beneath her red woolen cap, which sat cocked on her head in a rather provocative manner. The same shade of red emphasized lips that needed no highlighting for Joe to notice them.

"Come on. It's too cold to walk anywhere this morning," she urged him when he didn't immediately accept her offer.

It *was* too cold to walk the few blocks to the Mother Goose Land, but after what had happened last night, Sara was the last person he expected would be concerned about his comfort. He hesitated only a moment before he slid into the front seat of the station wagon, welcoming the blast of heat that greeted him.

"Thanks. I'm going to the Mother Goose Land to

pick up Nikki…or I guess you already know that since Jean was at your place this morning.''

''Oh, indeed she was, Joe,'' she said with a furtive grin. As the car pulled away from the curb, he heard the doors lock.

''You worried I'm going to fall out?'' he asked with a chuckle.

''Power locks. Happens automatically once the car's in gear so no kids fall out. It's my mother's wagon,'' she told him.

He removed his gloves and warmed fingers that had already started to go numb from the bitter cold. ''What is the temperature anyway?'' he asked, shoving his hands in front of the heating vent.

''I heard it was two,'' she answered.

''Two? No wonder I can't warm up.'' He shivered and continued to rub his hands together.

''What happened? You get soft living in that warm climate?'' There was no derision in her voice, just a teasing quality that sounded almost flirtatious.

''Doesn't the cold bother you? I mean, you've lived away from here nearly as long as I have.''

''Actually I find it a bit invigorating,'' she said, turning onto Main Street. She honked and waved at a woman going into the post office. The woman waved back and grinned. ''That's Dorothy Tottie. Remember her? She edited the school newspaper.''

''Dottie Tottie?''

Sara clicked her tongue in admonishment. ''She hated when kids called her that. Not that I blame her.''

''She's been here ever since we graduated?''

''Mom says she lived in Vargas for a while. She married Greg Roland…big, thick kid who played football.''

"The one who got caught stealing the pig from the Hendricks farm?"

Sara smiled. "That's the one. They have a couple of kids, but Greg never did quite outgrow his penchant for taking stuff that wasn't his. He stole another guy's wife and ended up getting shot. Dottie divorced him when he asked if she'd mind if his girlfriend moved in to help nurse him back to health."

She brought him up to date on the status of several other classmates as she drove past the once familiar landmarks of Christmas. The feed store, the old school, the church.

When she passed the Mother Goose Land, he said, "Sara, you missed Jean's place."

She didn't seem concerned and continued driving.

When she took a left onto the county road bisecting the town, he asked, "What are you doing? Giving me a tour of Christmas?"

"And what would be the point?" she asked, her eyes on the road.

"To try to convince me Christmas is worth saving."

She shot him a sideways glance. "I think that would be a waste of time, don't you?".

"Yes. All I want to do this morning is pick up my daughter and get out of town."

"You want out of town? I'll take you out of town," she said as she pulled onto the highway.

Warning bells went off in Joe's head. "Sara, what are you doing?"

"I'm taking you out of town," she stated with an annoying smugness, then stomped the gas pedal to the floor as she pulled out onto the highway.

"Sara, stop goofing around and take me to get Nikki," he ordered, trying not to sound panicky, although he was not feeling very calm at the way she was barreling down the road.

She ignored him.

"Sara, where are you going?"

"That's for me to know and you to find out," she said coyly.

"No, it's for me to know. I suggest you turn this car around and take me back to Jean's," he stated in no uncertain terms.

"Or you'll do what?" Again she shot him that sideways glance that was no longer cute, but annoying.

He reached for the door handle, but even if he were foolish enough to hop out of a station wagon traveling at fifty-five miles per hour, it would have been impossible. The automatic locks were activated.

"I don't know what game you think you're playing, but if this is your idea of a joke, you've had your little laugh for the day. Now take me back to Jean's."

She turned on the radio and music filled the car. A country version of "Jingle Bell Rock" brought a smile to her face as she hummed along with the melody.

"Sara, this is *not* funny."

"Gee, Joe. I seem to recall saying the same words to you one prom night ten years ago, and you know what you said to me?"

"Is that what this is about? Something that happened over ten years ago?"

She made a sound of disbelief, as if it were preposterous to even suggest such a thing. "Really, Joe, I may hold an occasional grudge now and then, but ten years?"

They were moving farther and farther away from town. "You want an apology, is that it? Okay, I apologize. I should have never kidnapped you the night of the prom. Now turn the car around.''

They rode past a meat market that had a life-size statue of a bull atop its roof. ''Look. There's Demming's Meat Market. I bet seeing that brings back a few memories, doesn't it?''

She was referring to the time he was suspended from school for being a part of a trio who managed to steal the bull and put it on the principal's front lawn. It had meant losing three days of school and being barred from attending the homecoming festivities, but he hadn't cared. It had been worth it to see the look on the principal's face when he had opened his door.

''You thought it was funny. Admit it,'' he coaxed her.

She couldn't prevent the smile that creased her cheeks. ''It was funny.''

Suddenly he was seventeen years old and full of pride at having impressed the most popular girl with his daring behavior. ''I knew you thought it was funny, even if you did look down your Goody Two-shoes nose at me as if I'd just landed from the Planet Moron.''

''Is that what you think? That I used to look down my nose at you?''

''You did, Sara.''

''I tried to be nice to you, Joe.''

Now he was the one who chuckled. ''Yeah, right.'' He looked out the window at the snow-covered land. Where *was* she taking him? ''It's really kind of you to want to give me a nostalgic trip down memory lane, but I need to get back to town. So just turn the car around and take me back.''

She sighed. ''I can't do that.''

Uneasiness knotted in his stomach. ''Why not?'' She

didn't answer him and he asked, "Sara, why are you doing this?"

"Maybe I just want to be with you, Joe."

The words came out sounding seductive. To his annoyance, he felt certain parts of his anatomy responding to the provocative statement. For one brief moment he wished she really meant those words, that she would tell him she had driven off with him because she found him irresistible.

It was a fantasy he couldn't afford. He reminded himself that with every mile they traveled, time was ticking away. Time he needed to get to the airport.

"And what about what I want, Sara?" he asked.

"Now, isn't that interesting? That's the same question I asked you the night you kidnapped me. And you know what you said to me?"

You're going to have trust me that I know what's best for you, Sara. I can show you a better time than you'll ever have at the dance. He was amazed that he could remember the words with such startling clarity. "I'm not having a good time, Sara."

"Maybe not…" She dangled the words provocatively.

"We're not seventeen and this isn't high school," he warned in a steely voice. "Now turn this car around and take me back to town."

"If I do that, Nikki will have to spend Christmas in California."

He stared at her is disbelief. "That's what this is about? Nikki staying here?"

"I told you she doesn't want to go home, Joe, but you wouldn't listen."

He groaned in frustration. "You're wrong about this.

I talked to her last night, and she told me she wants to spend Christmas with her cousins.''

"And you believed her?"

"Of course I believed her! I love my daughter and I want her to be happy. Don't you think if she wanted to stay here I'd let her stay?"

When she put on her blinker, he thought he had convinced her that he only wanted what was best for his daughter. Maybe Sara wasn't as stubborn as the rest of the town. He soon found out, however, that instead of using the dirt road as a place to turn around, she headed down the narrow tracks left by previous cars.

"Now where are you going?" he demanded.

"To a place where no one will find us."

Her words both excited and frustrated him. "All right. Enough is enough. This little kidnapping scheme has gone on long enough. Either you turn the car around or I'll do it for you," he threatened.

"I wouldn't advise you to do anything foolish, Joe."

"You're the one who's being foolish. Turn the car around," he repeated again.

"No."

The sight of her sitting behind the wheel acting if she were in control of the situation sent more than a tremor of excitement through him. He could see it in her eyes. They sparkled with exhilaration because she thought she had pulled a fast one on him. Well, he'd show her just who could outsmart whom.

He reached across to turn the ignition key off. But before his hand could reach the steering column, she pushed it away. What followed was a struggle—her right hand trying to fend off his left. It ended when he saw her face become ashen.

"Oh, my gosh!"

He looked out the windshield and saw the reason for her panic. A deer stood poised in the road.

She swerved to avoid hitting the animal and in the process skidded on a patch of ice that sent the station wagon careening out of control. Pumping the brakes proved useless as the car spun out and ended up in a snowdrift, the front end raised up higher than the back.

For several moments they both sat there in stunned silence. Then she cried out, "Now look what you made me do!" She shifted into reverse and tried to back the station wagon out of the drifted snow, but the car didn't move.

"Try rocking it," he instructed. "Shift back and forth between Reverse and Drive."

"I know how to rock a car out of the snow," she said irritably, but after repeatedly trying to jar the car free, she slumped over the wheel.

"Switch places with me and I'll try to get it out," he ordered. To his surprise she moved over so that he could come around to the driver's side. As he stepped out of the car, his foot sank deep into the snow. What was worse, as he trudged around to the driver's side, his boots sunk into a pool of icy cold water hidden beneath the snow.

As he climbed behind the wheel, he was wet, cold and so annoyed with Sara he could have easily read her the riot act. He didn't. He calmly tried rocking the car out of its predicament, but all he managed to do was bury the wheels deeper in the snow. After several minutes of spinning wheels, he, too, gave up.

"We're stuck," he spit out. "Stuck in the middle of nowhere." He pushed back the cuff of his jacket to look at his watch. "Just great. By the time we call someone to tow us out, I'll have to do about ninety to get to the airport on time. Where's your phone?''

"I don't have one."

His jaw dropped open. "You don't have a cell phone?''

"No. This isn't L.A. It's northern Minnesota."

He rolled his eyes heavenward. "That's why you should have one. You're in the middle of nowhere. What do you do if your car breaks down?"

She threw up her hands. "For crying out loud. Would you stop hollering at me? I'm not thrilled that we're stuck in a snowdrift any more than you are."

They both sat in silence for several moments. Then he asked, "Where were you going on this road anyway?"

"My brother has a lake cabin on Little Pine. It's only a little bit farther down this road."

"How much farther is it?"

She shrugged. "I suppose about a mile. We'll have to walk the rest of the way but at least it'll be warm there."

"And is there a phone?"

"No, but..."

He could only shake his head. "Then we might as well walk back to the highway. At least we'll be able to flag someone down."

"It's at least three or four miles back, and you're already wet." She glanced down at his legs.

He slapped his hands on the steering wheel and muttered an expletive. "None of this would have happened if you hadn't been so intent on getting revenge."

"I told you it wasn't revenge. I was thinking about Nikki." She opened the car door.

"Hey! Where are you going?" he demanded as she climbed out.

"I'm not going to sit here and listen to you holler at me."

She slammed the front door shut, then opened the rear one, leaning inside to pick up a thermos from the floor.

"Does that mean we have hot coffee?" he asked.

"*I* have hot coffee. And food."

He turned to see a picnic basket, also on the floor. "You really were planning on keeping me away, weren't you?"

She didn't answer him but pulled the picnic basket from the car.

He got out of the car and slammed his door shut. "You did all this because of Nikki?"

"She wants to stay here for Christmas."

"And she wants to be the first kid in space and she wants to ride on a magic carpet. Sara! Do you realize what you've done? We're going to miss our plane…the only plane that had any seats left on it," he nearly shouted in frustration. If he expected to see triumph in her eyes, he was mistaken. Caution, uncertainty, but not victory.

"If you want to walk to the highway, be my guest," she told him, buttoning the top of her jacket. "I'm going to the cabin. At least I won't freeze there. And I'll have food."

She started down the road carrying a heavy woolen blanket, the picnic basket and the thermos.

He pulled his gloves back on, raised the collar on his jacket and adjusted the Dodgers cap so that it was as low on his forehead as possible. By the time he waded through the knee-deep snow to the road, he was out of breath. He had to hurry to catch up with her.

"What's in here?" he asked, taking the picnic basket from her hands.

"Food. Are you hungry?"

"I will be if this walk doesn't get any easier. How far did you say we have to go?" He grimaced as he stared down the tree-lined road.

"Not far. At least you wore your Sorels," she said. "That baseball cap doesn't cover your ears."

"I was only going two blocks," he reminded her.

She reached inside her pocket and pulled out a headband. "Want this? You can use it to cover your ears and put your cap on over it. Better than getting frostbit."

The headband was a thick knitted circle of black with a pink stripe down the center. Reluctantly he accepted it from her outstretched hand and put it on.

As they started walking, she said, "You're more sensible than you were ten years ago. The Joe I knew back then would have never worn a woman's headband."

"No seventeen-year-old male would have worn a woman's headband," he remarked.

"True."

They walked in silence; the only sound was their boots crunching on the snow-covered road. Joe grew more irritable by the minute as the cold seemed to seep into every single joint in his body.

Finally he asked, "If we don't get somewhere fast we'll make the headlines on the news tonight. Man and woman found dead from exposure."

"It's not *that* cold," she contended.

"Your feet didn't step into a creek."

"We need to walk faster. Get your heart rate up so

you don't notice the cold," she told him, picking up the pace.

"How much farther is it?"

"You've asked that about five times," she told him.

"And you keep saying we're almost there. I'm almost frozen."

"Look. There it is."

It was a small strip of cedar sticking up out of the snow. The name Richards had been painted on it. Joe waded through thigh-high snow to reach the small log cabin hidden behind the trees.

"Quick. Give me the keys." He held out his hand as he stood on the step.

She reached in first one pocket, then the other. Panic widened her eyes.

"You do have the keys, right?"

She searched the pockets on her jacket, the pockets on her jeans, and Joe's anxiety increased. Then with a sly grin she reached inside the tiny zipper on her sleeve and pulled out a single key.

"Ta-daa! Had you scared, didn't I?"

She didn't give him the key but inserted it in the lock herself. Joe practically shouted for joy when the door opened.

Although the temperature inside the cabin was barely above freezing, at least it was out of the wind. And there was a fireplace with plenty of wood stacked next to it.

"We'd better get the fire going right away," she said, thinking along the same lines as him. "You do that and I'll see what's in the cupboards we can use."

It wasn't long before flames danced in the fireplace and Joe heaved a sigh of relief. "My jeans are soaked," he said, crouching in front of the crackling kindling.

"So are mine," Sara told him. "We should probably

take them off and let them dry. There are probably more blankets in the bedroom. Why don't you use this one and I'll get another.'' She handed him the plaid lap robe she had brought from the car.

He nodded, willing to do just about anything to warm up. While she was in the other room, he peeled the wet jeans away from his legs, setting them close to the fireplace. Then he wrapped the lap robe around his waist as if it were a sarong.

When Sara returned, she had an army-green blanket wrapped around her lower portion. She, too, set her jeans in front of the fireplace to dry. Over her shoulder was another blanket—this one blue—which she spread out on the floor.

"We might as well sit as close to the fire as possible," she told Joe.

So the two of them sat down on the floor with the picnic basket between them. Sara opened it and handed him a sandwich wrapped in plastic. "Ham and cheese on rye."

"You had this all planned, didn't you?"

"Not the skidding-off-the-road part," she answered. "Chips?"

He took the lunch-size bag of potato chips she offered.

Next she passed him the thermos. "There's something hot in here. Help yourself."

Joe unscrewed the cap and poured what looked to be whitened coffee. Only when he tasted the liquid, he realized that it was laced with alcohol.

"This is some potent coffee," he told her, the whiskey warming his insides quickly.

"I wanted to make sure I gave you the same opportunities you gave me," she told him with a sly grin.

"This isn't exactly strawberry wine," he argued.

"And I have no intention of getting you drunk," she countered.

"I didn't try to get you drunk. How was I to know you had never even had a sip of wine before? If I recall, it didn't take much for you to get a buzz on."

"I wouldn't have had anything to drink if you hadn't tricked me."

He made an exaggerated sound of disbelief. "You knew it wasn't strawberry pop when I gave it to you. The truth is you wanted to see what it was like to drink. Admit it. It was fun not being a Goody Two-shoes for just one night, wasn't it?"

"Why do you have to keep saying *Goody Two-shoes* as if it were an infectious disease?"

"There's nothing wrong with it except the whole town acted as if you could do no wrong."

"And that's why you really kidnapped me that night, wasn't it? You wanted to show the rest of the school that I was a big hypocrite. Pretending to be the nice girl in class, always following the rules, always doing what should be done."

Her voice rose in agitation.

"No, that's not what I wanted to do," he denied. "You know why I wanted you with me."

"Yeah, to ruin my reputation. Well, you succeeded."

"That's not why I did it and you know it," he argued.

She poured herself some of the Irish coffee. "It doesn't really matter, does it? It's over and done with."

"It mattered to me. Why can't you just admit that you enjoyed breaking a few rules that night?"

"All right. I liked the strawberry wine and I liked the fact that I didn't have to be the perfect student everybody looked up to. There. I've said it. Are you satisfied?''

She had taken off her hat so that her blond curls fell in a glorious disarray about her face. Her pale cheeks now had a rosy glow, thanks to the walk in the cold. Never had she looked more beautiful to Joe. He felt desire stir inside him and had to look away so that she wouldn't see it on his face.

''You're right. It's over and done with. There's no point in talking about that night.'' He scrunched up the sandwich wrapper and tossed it into the open basket. ''So what do we do next? Does anyone know we're out here?''

''Jean and your mother do,'' Sara admitted.

He shook his head. ''I should have known you'd have conspirators. I swear you could talk a thief into giving back the money he stole.''

''They understand what's important in life,'' she said with a lift of her chin.

''Meaning what? I don't?''

''Apparently not when it comes to your daughter. I told you last night I heard her talking to her mother…up in heaven.'' Her voice broke with emotion. ''She said it was the first time in three years that she wasn't lonely at Christmas and it was because she had found a place where everyone was nice to her.''

''Everyone's nice to her in California, too.''

''Are you sure?''

''Yes.'' Now he was the one who was on the defensive. ''She has family there—family she's very fond of, including her cousins.''

''Shawna and Lindsey.''

''She told you about them?''

"She's told me a lot of stuff," she said in what sounded like a sanctimonious tone to Joe.

"That doesn't make you an authority on what is best for my daughter."

"I didn't say I was."

"No, you're just trying to *help*. Boy, you really haven't changed, have you?"

"And what's that supposed to mean?"

"Always championing the underdog. You were never happy unless you were championing some lost cause. Now you've added my daughter to your list of causes."

"If you're trying to make me feel bad, it's not working," she told him, pouring herself a second cup of the coffee.

He grabbed the thermos when she had finished and refilled his own cup. "What I want to know is how did I miss out on all this goodwill?"

"I don't know what you mean."

"I was the biggest underdog in the whole town. How come you didn't make me your cause?"

She chuckled. "You didn't need my help, Joe. You were the coolest guy in class and you knew it."

"Not cool enough for the prom queen." He leaned closer to her.

She didn't back away. "I had a steady boyfriend."

He chuckled sardonically. "Elmer Fudd."

"There's nothing wrong with being a farm boy. And his name was Roger."

"It's not the farm that made him a doofus," Joe assured her.

She tried to hide her grin but couldn't. "He married Gina Dobbin."

"You're kidding."

She shook her head. "They have four kids. All boys."

"See? You could have broken up with him and dated me."

"No, I couldn't," she disagreed. "It wouldn't have been right. Besides, he was a nice guy. *He* never made me do anything I didn't want to do."

He could see that she was feeling the effects of the Irish cream. Her cheeks were still rosy despite the warmth in the cabin. Whenever she answered him, she had this lazy grin that reminded him of that night they had drunk strawberry wine. And just like that night, he found it charming.

"I didn't make you do anything you didn't want to do," he said softly.

"Hmmph." She tried to sound indignant, but failed. "In one night I did more with you than I had done in two years with Elmer. I mean Roger."

"As I said, he was a doofus."

She reached for a cookie. "He was a gentleman."

Joe chuckled. "So you keep telling me. How much Irish cream did you put in this stuff, anyway?" he asked, lifting his cup.

"Not that much. Why?"

"You're getting a buzz on."

She giggled. "I am not."

"Yes, you are. I recognize the signs. You're grinning. And flirting with me."

Again she giggled. "I never flirt. I'm not interested in men anymore."

"Really."

"Really. One ex-husband is more than enough for me, thank you," she said primly.

"He was that bad?" He didn't know what made him

ask. It was none of his business and if he were wise, he wouldn't make it any of his business. But when it came to Sara Richards he wasn't a wise man.

"He would make Dottie's ex look like a Boy Scout."

"He was unfaithful?"

"I discovered—*after the ceremony*—that *true blue* were not words in his vocabulary."

The thought of her being hurt by some jerk of a guy evoked feelings of anger inside him. "Then the marriage was a mistake."

She shrugged. "It happens to people all the time. Happily-ever-after is a rarity."

"That's rather cynical for the girl who told the senior class at graduation that anything was possible if we just believed in ourselves."

"I did believe in myself. I just shouldn't have believed in him." There was a cynicism in her voice he had never heard there before.

"One bad apple shouldn't spoil the whole crate."

"Theater apples are different from corporate apples. My parents warned me about marrying an actor, told me it wouldn't be an easy life."

"He was an actor?"

She nodded. "I met him while I was going to school. He was in the play, I was working on the costumes."

"He was from around here?"

She shook her head. "From South Dakota. Before either of us had graduated, he went off to New York for a chance at the big time. I followed him. The rest is, as they say, history."

It bothered him that she left Christmas for a guy who wasn't faithful, but when he had asked her to go away with him, she had turned him down. He at least, wouldn't have ever been untrue to her.

''Now I'm back right where I started.'' She stared at her bare left hand, as if remembering that at one time there had been a wedding band on her finger. ''You probably think I wanted to move back to Christmas. That I wanted to try to save the town from going ka-put.''

''Didn't you?''

She shook her head. ''I only came home because I had no place else to go. So you see, I don't want to be here any more than you do.'' She smiled at him then. ''It's kinda funny, isn't it? I mean, here we both are, neither one of us exactly thrilled to be spending Christmas in Christmas....''

''I don't plan on spending Christmas here,'' he told her.

She stared at him over her cup. ''You gonna charter a plane home?''

''I'm a determined man, Sara. You ought to know I always get what I want.'' He turned his attention to the fire, adding another log to maintain its intensity.

''Would it be so awful to spend Christmas here?'' she asked when he sat back down.

''And watch my mom and Sam Hanson play kissy-face?''

''Does it bother you that she wants to play kissy-face?''

''No,'' he quickly denied. Then, seeing her quirk an eyebrow in disbelief, he said, ''All right. Maybe it does a little. My father's been gone over twenty years. She's never been interested in anyone in all that time.''

''Maybe she just never found anyone who could hold a candle to him,'' she said softly.

He sipped his coffee thoughtfully. ''Maybe.''

"Sam's a nice man. They make a cute Mr. and Mrs. Claus," she commented.

"That doesn't mean they'd make a cute Mr. and Mrs."

"You still haven't told me why it's so important that you go back to California for Christmas."

"Because it's home to me."

She sighed. "I'm sorry you never felt that way about this town."

"Do you think many people do? I mean, the population at one time was up over a thousand. Now it's what? Not quite three hundred?"

"That's not because they don't like it here. As the businesses left, so did their jobs. Many were forced to leave to find employment."

"Which is a natural occurrence and the very reason why you shouldn't be putting all this effort into trying to save the town from going under. Sara, you're trying to put a Band-Aid on a wound that's been hemorrhaging for years."

"A Band-Aid will at least stop the bleeding for now. It's not like we haven't thought of the future, Joe. We realize that what the town really needs is a plan for economic redevelopment."

"And how do you hope to accomplish that?" He managed to keep the skepticism from his voice.

"We have another campaign planned."

He rolled his eyes. "Now why doesn't that surprise me?"

"We're going to offer economic incentives for businesses to relocate here."

This time he couldn't prevent the sarcasm from coming out. "You have no money. What are you going to use?"

"Land."

He threw back his head and laughed. "This is northern Minnesota, not the city."

"Go ahead and laugh all you want. It's worked for other small towns." She rattled off a list of cities that had been revitalized through such a program.

"Those cities had a tax base to start with. Sara, trust me on this. I know what I'm talking about. You're on a dead horse."

She dismissed him with a flap of her hand. "Oh, what do you know? You're just some stuffy numbers cruncher who lives in la la land."

"Numbers cruncher?" he repeated, amused by her description of his job.

"You deal with investing money for people who make an obscene amount of money in the entertainment world. How would you know what works for small-town America?"

He knew there was no point in arguing his credentials with her.

"You know, Joe, it's probably a good thing we never got together when we were teenagers. We're worlds apart."

"We shouldn't be. You've lived in New York City. You're not small-town anymore," he told her.

"That doesn't mean I can't understand what it means to these people to lose something they believe in. And trust me, New York isn't all it's cracked up to be, either."

"You just said you're here in Christmas against your will."

"I am, but I don't want to be in New York, either. I don't know where I want to be. I guess I don't really fit in anywhere anymore." Her voice broke, and then a tear trickled down her cheek. She swiped at it with the back of her hand. "Oh, shoot. You were right. I did drink too much of the coffee. Now I'm getting weepy."

"And I haven't even kissed you."

They both knew what he was talking about. On the night of the prom the strawberry wine had chased away her outrage at being kidnapped, leaving her in a tipsy state that had her giggling and flirting with him as if she didn't have a care in the world. They had danced and nearly made love, only to have her end up crying.

"I didn't cry that night because of—of…that," she stammered.

"No?"

"No. I felt bad because I was thinking we should have been able to go to the prom together instead of spending the night in the back of a bar."

"You turned me down when I asked you."

"I know. Because of Roger."

"And you couldn't hurt him."

She shook her head.

"And what if you knew then what you know now…would you have said yes when I asked you?" Suddenly the question seemed very important.

"I wish I had said yes. Because instead of dancing in the back of a bar we should have been doing the grand march in the school gym and all the girls would have been jealous because I was with the coolest guy in class…instead of Elmer Fudd." As if suddenly embarrassed by her admission, she started putting stuff back into the picnic hamper.

As she leaned over, the blanket she had wrapped around her leg parted, revealing a generous amount of thigh and a glimpse of pink satin. Joe's heartbeat accelerated. Seeing the direction of his gaze, she tried to tug the ends of the blanket together.

His hand stopped hers. ''Don't cover them. They're great-looking legs, Sara.'' Unable to resist, he slid his hand inside the woolen blanket, placing it on her warm flesh.

The sudden intake of breath told him his touch was as electric to her as it was to him.

''What are you doing?'' Her question sounded airy and tentative.

He moved his hand across the smooth skin of her thigh. ''Your skin is hot.''

She licked her lips and this time Joe was the one who had a sharp intake of breath. He continued his exploration of her leg, watching the play of emotions on her face.

''I never forgot what it was like to touch you,'' he murmured huskily.

''Joe, we shouldn't....'' she began, but her eyes contradicted her protest. As did the tiny little sighs she emitted as his hands moved across her flesh.

''That night we spent at the Stable...it was the only time I felt as if I belonged in Christmas,'' he told her, loving the feel of her skin beneath his fingertips.

''Oh, Joe,'' she said on a sigh of delight as his fingers continued their journey toward the satin bikini briefs. Slowly they traveled to that forbidden destination, encouraged by the look in her eyes. Before they could reach it, however, she grabbed him by the shoulders and covered his mouth with hers in a kiss that caught him by surprise.

For almost a week he had been wondering what it would be like to hold her in his arms, to feel those luscious lips on his, to taste the sweetness he remembered from so many years ago. Now she was there and it was every bit as wonderful as he had remembered.

Actually it was better. Her mouth was warm and soft beneath his, responding to his lips with an urgency that fueled the fire of desire burning inside of him. Ten years ago he had kissed a girl. Now he was with a woman and it showed in her every move as her tongue boldly invaded his mouth, intimately conveying a message he needed to receive.

Her hands pulled him closer, smoothing the ruffled hairs at the back of his neck, massaging the muscles of his shoulder, arousing him as no other woman had ever been able to do. With every thrust of her tongue inside his mouth, he could feel the remaining threads of willpower slipping away as desire took control of his thoughts and actions.

It had been a long time since he had been with a woman, and his body begged him to take what she so willingly offered. It was one of the things he had loved about Sara ten years ago, that she gave of her heart and soul when she was in his arms. That much hadn't changed.

Needing to feel even closer to her, he lowered her onto the floor so that they lay side by side in front of the fire. He slowly unwrapped the blanket from around her waist, awed by the beautiful sight she made lying half-naked beside him.

"Aren't you going to going to take off yours?" she asked with a look in her eye that told him if he didn't want to remove it, she would.

He grinned as he whipped the woolen blanket away from his bare legs. Her eyes darkened at the sight of him in his briefs.

"See what you do to me?" he murmured, then covered her lips once more, kissing them with an intensity that had every nerve in his body throbbing with desire.

Just as his hand had explored the silky softness of her skin, hers made the same journey up his thigh, causing tremors to rack Joe's body. Teasingly they caressed his flesh until they found the bulge in his briefs. He groaned then, at the ecstatic feelings her caresses created.

"You're burning me up," he said in between kisses.

"I don't know how you do what you do to me, Joe, but it is so good," she moaned as she arched her body against his.

She seemed just as eager to take it to the next step, her eyes glowing with passion, her lips swollen from the pressure of their kisses. She purred as he brushed fingers across the V between her legs, then smiled as he slipped his fingers inside the silky underwear. One minute they were consumed with kissing and caressing, the next she was pushing him away.

At first Joe didn't understand why, but then he heard the sound of a fist pounding on wood.

"There's someone at the door." Sara was the one who stated the obvious.

They both scrambled to their feet, frantically wrapping the blankets around their waists. Joe was the one to answer the door.

Standing on the front porch was a tall man wearing a cap with ear flaps, a large parka and leather mittens. Joe should have been glad to see they had been rescued. Should have been. One glance back at Sara told him there was no way he could be happy to see anyone at the moment.

"I saw the car down the road. I'm Frank Feester. Is

everything all right?'' he gave Joe a rather suspicious look.

Before Joe knew it, Sara was at his side. "Hi, Frank. Remember me? Sara Richards?"

They exchanged brief greetings and she added, "I went off the road…saw a deer. It's a good thing you came by. With no phone, we could have been here for a while," she said, which didn't make Joe happy. She sounded almost relieved that they were being rescued. She, the one who had done her best to keep him away from town.

"I've got a four-wheel drive. I can get you out if you want," he offered.

Joe exchanged glances with Sara, but didn't say a word. If she was ready to leave, then she would be the one to make the decision. After all, she could tell him to call Christmas and have them send a tow truck. Later. Much later. If she wanted.

Apparently she didn't want to because she said, "That would be good. Just give us a few minutes here to put out the fire and get our things together." She giggled shyly and blushed as Frank's eyes saw that neither was wearing pants. "Our jeans were wet. We had to take them off and try to dry them in front of the fire."

Frank looked as if they had told him an alien had landed and stolen their car. Instead of going back to his truck, he waited inside for the two of them to change. Only minutes ago Joe and Sara had been like two lovers, at ease with each other's half-naked bodies. Now they were as uncomfortable as two strangers. And with the older man in the cabin, there was no way they could talk about what had just happened between them.

Joe hoped that she would at least whisper something

to him in an aside. She didn't. Which was just fine with him. She could pretend she hadn't melted in his arms and wanted to make love to him. He knew differently.

As they left the cabin he told himself it was a good thing Sara was acting as if nothing had happened between them. He was going back to California if he had to hitchhike to get there, and the sooner he forgot about Christmas and everyone in the tiny town, the better.

Chapter Seven

"She's hung up but good. You're going to have to get a tow," Frank Feester told Sara when it became apparent that no amount of effort on his part was going to get the station wagon out of the ditch.

"Thank you for trying, Frank," Sara said as he unhooked the chain connecting the two vehicles.

"There's an old fence running along that ditch. Looks to me like you're hooked on one of the posts," he said as he got to his feet and threw the thick coil of chain into the back of the pickup.

"Where's the closest service station that will send out a tow truck?" Joe asked.

"That'd be Fritz's back in Christmas," Frank answered. "Hop in and I'll give you a ride back to town."

"No, that's all right. If you'll just take us to the nearest phone, we won't need to take up any more of your time," Joe said.

"That'd be in Christmas, too. I got a CB in the truck. I can contact the missus and she can call someone for you, but you're going to get pretty cold waiting out here for someone to come."

"We'll take the ride," Sara finally spoke up, annoyed

that Joe acted as if he were in charge. After all, it was her car, not his.

"Just let me make room," Frank said, opening the door to the cab where he had to move a pile of stuff that included an ice-fishing bucket, tip-ups and a bag of minnows. The ice bucket and tip-ups he threw in the back, but the minnows he handed to Sara. "Hold these, will you? They'll freeze in the back."

Sandwiched between Frank Feester and Joe, holding a plastic bag with shiners swimming inside was not how Sara had expected to return to town that afternoon. Besides being trapped between two distinctive scents—tobacco on her left and cologne on her right—she had to snake her legs around the stick shift, which made it impossible not to bump against Joe as the aging pickup rumbled down the snow-rutted road.

Fortunately Frank kept up a steady conversation about the trials and tribulations of winter in Minnesota. Sara didn't dare look at Joe. Not after what had happened between them at the cabin. She had been avoiding his eyes ever since Frank had put a stop to their unexpected passionate encounter.

She tried to focus on the road, looking straight ahead and not at him, but her eyes were drawn to his hands. They were folded in his lap, holding his leather gloves. Absently his thumb rubbed the rough suede fabric, and Sara was reminded of how that thumb had rubbed across her breast. A shiver of longing ricocheted through her.

"You cold?" Frank asked.

"No, I'm fine," she answered, hoping the heat that was warming her limbs wouldn't send a flush to her cheeks.

"So what are you doing for a living these days?" Frank asked Joe.

"I'm in finance," he answered.

Sara could tell by the brevity of his answer that he didn't want to expand on just what it was he did in finance, but Frank was a curious guy.

"You a loan officer?"

"No. That would be banking. I'm on the stocks-and-bonds end of things," he replied.

"Then I don't suppose you could get your bank in California to help us do a little creative financing so we can keep Christmas running," Frank said.

Sara was as interested in Joe's answer as Frank was. She should have known it would be as smooth as silk.

"You can be sure that if there were a way for me to help, my mother would have come up with it," Joe said with a knowing grin.

Frank chuckled. "You're right about that. She's been the steam behind this whole town project for quite some time now."

Sara's eyes finally met Joe's. Without saying a word she told him, "So there. I'm vindicated." Aloud, she couldn't resist saying, "If our Victorian Christmas celebration goes as we've planned, we won't need any bank loans."

As she expected, Joe stiffened beside her. Frank took the opportunity to ask her about the fund-raiser, which was now only two days away. She took great pleasure in answering his questions, knowing perfectly well that the entire subject was a source of irritation for Joe.

Why she wanted to irritate him she wasn't sure. Maybe it was because he hadn't so much as tried to utter one word about what had happened between them at the cabin. Not that he had the opportunity to discuss it with her, but he could have at least whispered something in her ear to let her know that it had meant something to him other than a way to pass the time. He hadn't said one word to her about the way they had kissed and touched each other. For all Sara knew, she had simply been a diversion. Not a pleasant thought to someone who didn't take romance lightly.

The minute Frank's truck pulled into the service station—which was right across the street from the Mother Goose Land—Nikki came running across the street, the golden retriever at her heels.

"Dad! You're back! Grandma's been worried ever since she heard Sara almost hit a deer with the car."

"I'm sure that's not all your grandmother's been worrying about," he said with a sideways glance at Sara.

"Are we still gonna go home today?" Nikki wanted to know.

"I'm not sure," he answered. "I need to make some phone calls. Whose dog is that?"

"Nobody's. Sara's taking care of her until we can find her a home." She petted the dog's neck lovingly. "Isn't she sweet?"

"Nikki, we already have a dog. You should give her back so we can go back to Grandma's."

"I have to go back to Auntie Jean's first and put my stuff away. She's been showing me how to make lace angels. I've made three of them so far." She turned to Sara. "I've got one for you, Sara. Should I bring it over to your house later?"

"Why don't you go get it right now and give it to Sara?" Joe suggested.

"But I'm not sure the glue's dried. Can't we stay

until tomorrow? Then I could finish making one for Shawna.''

Joe shifted from foot to foot and looked about impatiently. It was obvious that all he wanted was to get out of Christmas and get out fast. Their romantic interlude had meant nothing to him. Sara had to swallow back her disappointment. All the way home in the truck she had hoped that once they arrived back in Christmas he'd make some effort to talk to her, but it was now obvious that wasn't going to happen.

"Don't worry about it, Nikki," Sara spoke up. "I can get it from Jean later."

"But I want to give it to you myself." She turned back to her father. "Even if we do leave today, we can still stop by and say goodbye to Sara, can't we?"

He sighed. "All right. Now we really need to get back to Grandma's." He held out his hand for hers. "Come, but leave the dog here."

Before she took his hand, she bent down to give the golden a hug. "Bye, Kris. You stay and be good for Sara, okay?" With a wave to Sara she headed off down the street with her father.

Unfortunately the dog didn't want to stay with Sara. It trailed behind Nikki. Joe tried to send her back to Sara, but the golden was persistent.

Sara whistled, but it did no good. "Just ignore her, Nikki. She'll find her way back to my house," she called out to the child, who tried to point the dog in Sara's direction.

It was useless. The dog was determined to follow Nikki. Sara watched the golden brush up against Joe's leg. To her surprise he stopped to pet the dog. She could see Nikki pleading with her father, his head shaking. Then Nikki came running back toward Sara.

She was out of breath, her eyes wide. "Can Kris sleep at my grandma's house tonight? My dad says it's okay."

"Sure, if you think your grandma won't mind."

"She won't."

"Okay."

As the youngster raced back toward her father, Sara thought, *So you're not such a bad guy after all, are you, Joe Gibson?*

JOE KNEW he should never have come back to Christmas. Nothing good had happened since he'd been here. And today...well, today should have been a clear message that going back to California was something he needed to do and do soon.

If he closed his eyes, he could still feel Sara's lips on his. Soft, warm, tempting. She had tricked him into missing his plane and what had he done? Taken her in his arms and nearly made love with her.

The memory caused him to ache with longing. She stirred feelings in him best left unstirred. All that talk about her ex... He raked a hand through his hair. She aroused his protective instincts—and a few other instincts that had nothing to do with keeping her safe. The question was why? She was from his past—a past he wanted to ignore. And she had broken his heart. So why after ten years did she still evoke such strong feelings in him?

It was a question he thought was better left unanswered. As soon as he walked into his mother's kitchen, he picked up the phone and called the airlines. It was just as he expected. Every seat to L.A. was taken.

So Sara had won. Or so she thought. Until he remembered the name of a client who had once told him that if he ever found himself in a pinch with the airlines to give him a call. He flipped open his day planner. With one phone call he found a solution to his travel problems.

As he hung up the receiver he smiled to himself. It paid to have friends in the right places. A client had managed to get him on a private jet.

And not just any private jet, but one belonging to a celebrity. An actor with roots in St. Paul who would be spending Christmas Eve day in Minnesota, then flying to California that evening. He agreed to let Nikki and Joe fly back with him.

All they had to do was be at the airport by six o'clock on the twenty-fourth of December. They'd be back in California before Santa could put on his suit and say ho-ho-ho to Shawna and Lindsey.

When he told his mother of the opportunity, she wasn't pleased. "So, you're really going to leave, even after everything that's happened?"

"By *everything,* you mean Sara's attempt to kidnap me and keep me from leaving?" He met her gaze with a glare of his own.

His mother didn't look the least bit sheepish at having been found out. "I helped her because it was the right thing to do."

Joe could only shake his head in disbelief. "You honestly believe that?"

"Yes, I do." She glanced into the living room to make sure her granddaughter was still watching television and not about to walk into the room. "Nikki wants to stay," she said in a near whisper.

"So you and Sara keep telling me. What I don't understand is why Nikki doesn't tell me."

"Have you asked her?"

"Yes. Right before dinner. She said the same thing she's said every time I've asked. 'I wish we could be both places, Dad.' She made it very clear to me that she doesn't want to miss Christmas with her cousins, either. Mom, ever since Angela died I've tried to make the holidays as painless as possible for her. She needs to be with Angela's family. That's why I'm taking her back."

"For a smart man you're awfully obtuse at times," his mother retorted.

He sighed. "Mom, I know you want her with you, but I think it's better that she spend Christmas in California."

"Better for whom? You? Are you sure you're not using Nikki to get away from the bad memories you have of this town?"

"No."

"I sure hope not," she said quietly. "You can be a stubborn man at times."

"Like mother, like son, I guess," he shot back at her.

She gasped in annoyance. "Why are you so ornery? Didn't you eat today?"

He chuckled. "Sara brought a lunch for us. Of course, you already knew that, didn't you. You set me up."

"And as I said, for a good reason." With those words she marched out of the room, pausing only to say, "And by the way, Sara called to say you still have her headband. She wants it back."

Sara. Was there no escaping hearing her name? Throughout dinner it had seemed to him that every other sentence his mother and daughter uttered had included her name. And it didn't help that he couldn't stop thinking about her. Or those beautiful legs that had felt oh so smooth and had tempted him… He deliberately pushed such thoughts from his mind.

But before he went to bed that night, he couldn't resist pulling the knit headband from his jacket pocket and lifting it to his nose. There was a hint of that tropical scent he had smelled in her hair. He slipped the headband in place, then set his Dodgers cap on his head and glanced in the mirror.

He looked ridiculous. Yet Sara hadn't so much as cracked a smile when he had put the thing on his head.

He pulled it off and shoved it back into his pocket. Tomorrow he'd send it over with Nikki. He didn't need to see Sara again. All she had done was annoy him since he'd been home—and remind him of feelings better left undisturbed. Of all the people he had known in his life, she had always created the most turmoil with his emotions.

He was not a happy man as he prepared for bed. That was because he knew every obstacle he had encountered in Christmas had been created by Sara. If it wasn't for her crusade to save the town, his mother would be going back to California with him. But that wasn't going to happen now because Sara had managed to bamboozle his mother into feeling so guilty about the town's troubles that she was willing to give up spending Christmas with her granddaughter. And now even Nikki was dangerously close to succumbing to Sara's charm.

The more he thought about it, the more irritated he became. There was only one solution. Get out of Christmas and forget that she had ever been his first love. And that he wanted her so badly he ached every time he thought about her.

December 21, 3:00 p.m.

"ALICE, IT'S EUGENIA. I'm calling about Joe and Sara."

"You've heard?"

"About what happened yesterday? Yes."

"Thanks to Frank Feester, I think everybody's heard."

"Nothing happened."

"Of course not."

"Sara said it was just a kiss."

"That's what Joe said, too," Alice told her. "Do you believe them?"

"No. Do you?"

"Uh-uh. I've only seen Joe this ornery one other time."

"The day after the prom?"

"Uh-huh. What about Sara?"

"She's been dragging herself around the house. Says she thinks she's catching a cold, but I have another diagnosis for her condition."

"The love bug?"

"She's got all the signs. Mooning around here, staring off into space with that dreamy look in her eyes."

"So what do you think we should do about it?"

"Do? Oh, we can't do anything. Can we?"

"I don't see why not."

"I promised myself I'd never be one of those matchmaking mothers."

"And as tempting as it's been, I've never once stuck my nose into Joe's life. Even though it's been three years and Nikki does need a mother."

"She's such a lovely child and she does seem to be very fond of Sara."

"Oh, she is. She talks about her constantly."

"Maybe we should get Sara to take Nikki ice skating."

"Joe loves to skate—or at least he did when he was a kid."

"When's he planning to leave for California?"

"Soon. We'll need to work fast...."

December 22, 1:00 p.m.

JOE HAD JUST FINISHED polishing up his old hockey skates when the doorbell rang. Since his mother was gone and Nikki was upstairs, he had no choice but to answer it.

Sara stood on the front porch, a pair of skates slung over her shoulder. Immediately his blood began to race through his veins.

"I didn't expect to see you," he said to her after she had said hello.

"I've come to take Nikki ice skating. Is she ready?"

"There must have been a misunderstanding. I'm taking Nikki skating this afternoon."

Joe knew the minute the words had left her mouth that he had been set up by his mother.

"But your mother told me to come by at one...."

He rubbed the back of his neck with his hand. "I think she got her signals crossed."

Just then Nikki came bouncing down the stairs in her purple jacket. "Sara, hi! Are you coming skating with us, too? Awesome! Dad, this is going to be so much fun! Sara's coming, too!" She jumped up and down like a jack-in-the-box.

Joe looked at Sara, who lifted her eyebrows expressively. He could see that she didn't want to have to tell his daughter there had been a mistake. Neither one wanted to put a pin in Nikki's bubble, which is what would have happened had one of them backed out of the ice skating. Joe knew it was exactly what his mother was counting on happening.

So the three of them went to the skating rink at the park. As much as Joe hated to admit it, Sara was the perfect person to teach his daughter to skate. She had the patience and the skill necessary to get Nikki started. Other than skating fast to get the hockey puck in the net, he hadn't taken any time to learn the finer art of figure skating as a kid, but Sara had, and she impressed him, as well as Nikki, with her graceful movements on the ice.

Once Nikki had mastered staying on her feet, she refused to take a break. While Joe and Sara sat on a park bench resting their tired ankles, she continued to skate across the ice, making friends with a couple of other girls who were skating.

"You're a good teacher, Sara," Joe said sincerely as they watched Nikki cut across the ice with the others.

"I had a good pupil."

"Nikki's become very fond of you."

"She's a lovely child, Joe," she said, waving at Nikki as she passed by.

"You like kids, don't you?"

She looked at him then and said, "Yes, I do. Why would you think I didn't?"

He shrugged. "No particular reason, I guess."

"It would have been reckless for me to have had children with my ex-husband. We didn't have a good marriage," she stated a bit defensively.

"You'll get no argument from me on that one," he assured her, wishing there weren't such a tension between them every time they were together. Unfortunately it seemed the only way to dispel it was to kiss her, but that was something he couldn't do. Not in front of Nikki.

"So tell me," he urged her. "Has that bad experience tainted your views on love and marriage?"

"No. I still want to have a family some day."

Of course she did. Because she was a loving and compassionate woman. And Joe knew she would make a good mother. The realization hit him like a ton of bricks.

"Why are you looking at me so funny?" she wanted to know.

"I'm not," he denied, quickly looking away so she wouldn't have a clue as to what was going through his head. He was grateful when Nikki finally did tire and asked if they could go inside the warming house for some refreshments.

What he didn't need was to think of Sara as a mother for his daughter. Just because she was good to Nikki didn't mean she would be good for him. The past was proof of that. She had promised him she'd be his true love only to tell him she had been wrong to make such a promise.

No, Sara was small-town and he was big-city. Their worlds were far apart, and nothing in the past ten years had changed the fact that he was still the boy who wasn't good enough for her.

He needed to remember that for two more days and forget about how good it had been to kiss her at the cabin. It wouldn't be easy, but he would do it. Because he wasn't going to return to California with a broken heart.

December 23, 7:00 p.m.

"YOU WANT TO ADD some Heet to your gas tank? It's going below zero tonight."

Joe looked at the high-school kid pumping gas into his rented Explorer.

"Yeah. Heet would be good," he said, handing the kid a twenty-dollar bill. "Keep the change."

"Thanks!"

Joe remembered what it was like to pump gas when the air was so cold you thought your hand would freeze to the metal handle before you were finished. On his way home he tuned in the local radio station to hear what the weather would be like tomorrow.

"So if you've got travel plans for the holidays, you'll probably be cold, but the roads should be in pretty good driving conditions as long as you're going south," the voice on the airwaves reported.

South was the direction Joe was heading. Not that it mattered. The Explorer had four-wheel drive. It could navigate the winter roads with ease.

Later that evening he sat upstairs in his room with his laptop open. He didn't realize how late it was until he glanced at his watch and saw that it was almost midnight. He closed the file on the screen and went to pull the shade on the window. As he did, he noticed snowflakes falling.

It was just a light dusting of flurries. As much as he hated to admit it, it made the town look postcard perfect. A sprinkling of lights lit windows edged with frost, smoke curled from chimney stacks, rooftops glistened with snow.

It was peaceful and quiet. So different from the world where he had spent the past ten years.

The longer he watched, the more mesmerized he became by the snowflakes that swirled outside his window. Before long the wind began to whistle through the eaves, and he saw fewer houses, fewer lights.

Before turning in, he went downstairs and flipped on the television. An old rerun of *Gunsmoke* had James Arness strutting his cowboy stuff. He channel surfed, looking for the weather channel. It didn't take him long to realize there was no weather channel. He was about to turn the television off when a tiny beeping sound alerted him to a message scrolling from right to left across the bottom of the screen.

It was a national weather advisory for a winter-storm warning. Four to six inches of snow were expected for the counties highlighted in red in the Minnesota graphic at the bottom right corner of the screen. Christmas was right on the border of the counties affected by the warning.

"That can't be right," he muttered to himself. Just a few hours ago he had heard the weather report on the radio. No snow was in the forecast.

He sat through a second scrolling of the same information. It hadn't changed. Christmas was expected to get four to six inches of snow.

How could they get six inches when it was so cold? Didn't storms need moisture in the air, moisture that came from the meeting of cold and warm air? Not that he would know. It was true he had spent his youth in Minnesota but he had never paid any attention to the explanations given for heavy snows. As a kid he had welcomed the warnings and blizzard conditions because it had meant the chance for a school closing.

He got up and went to look out the window one more time. He could see his mother's outdoor thermometer tacked to the ledge. It read seven below zero.

He looked at his watch. Even if he had the number

to the travel center, there wouldn't be anybody there at this time of night. There was nothing to do but go to bed and hope the forecasters were wrong.

They weren't. When he awoke the next morning, it was still snowing. He let the curtain slip back into place with a groan. How much of the white stuff was out there was anybody's guess.

Before showering or shaving, he went downstairs to turn on the television. Only his mother had beat him to it. She sat on the edge of her rocker, her hands folded beneath her chin.

"We're in a winter-storm warning. We're supposed to get eight to twelve inches or more," she said solemnly.

"Twelve? Last night it was four to six. Now it's eight to twelve?" Joe groaned and sat down on the sofa.

"They're saying no travel is advised anyway in the northern third of the state." Her voice was nearly tearful. "What are we going to do?"

"Where's the travel line number?" he asked, getting to his feet. "I'll call and see what condition the roads are in south of here. Driving to the airport might not be a problem."

"South of here? That's all you're worried about it? Getting out of here?" She looked at him as if he were seventeen and had just uttered a cuss word in her presence. "Joe, if Highway 75 is closed, our Victorian Christmas celebration will be a flop. All our work will have been for nothing!"

"Just get me the number, Mom, and I'll find out what I can," he said calmly.

She fluttered about the kitchen, opening drawers, checking notepads and then finally produced a scrap of green paper. While he dialed, she hovered anxiously at his side.

"It's bad," he said as he hung up the phone. "They've closed several of the highways in the area because the plows can't see to stay on the road. Snow's blowing and drifting too badly." That brought a gasp from his mother's mouth.

"I better wake up Nikki," he said, heading for the stairs.

"You're not thinking of starting out in this, are you?" she asked, trailing behind him.

"You heard the weather-service report. It's worse in northern Minnesota. I think once we get headed south of here we'll be fine." He took the stairs two at a time.

"Have you looked outside?" she called after him, following his footsteps.

"Please, Mother, I don't need any lectures."

"I don't want you to take my granddaughter on the roads when they're reporting treacherous driving conditions." She followed Joe into her bedroom, where Nikki sat on the floor next to the golden.

"Dad, I think there's something wrong with Kris. She's acting kinda strange."

"Don't worry about Kris. I need you to get dressed so we can leave," he told her.

"But you said we weren't going until noon. That I could go to the Victorian Christmas celebration for a little bit."

"Plans have changed. It's snowing." He turned to his mother and said, "I'm going to shower. See that she gets ready, will you?"

"Dad, wait!" Joe stopped and waited for Nikki to speak. "I can't miss the Victorian Christmas celebration!"

"Nikki, if we don't leave soon, we're not going to get out of here."

She looked out at the snow coming down. "Maybe it wouldn't be so bad to spend Christmas here."

He sat down beside her and reached for her delicate hands. "Are you saying you don't want to go back to California today?"

She nodded soberly. "I like it here, Dad. I'm sorry. I know you don't want to stay, but maybe this snow is a sign that we're supposed to be here with Grandma and not with Shawna and Lindsey."

Joe felt as if someone had taken the wind out of his sails. He had put so much effort into getting back to California and it hadn't even been necessary. Sara and his mother had been right.

"You're not mad at me, are you, Dad?" she asked, glancing up at him with a look that was very similar to the one Kris gave him every time he tried to put her outside.

He hugged her close and said, "No, I'm not mad. You're probably right. This snow just might be a sign that we shouldn't leave. Besides, we wouldn't want to worry Grandma, would we?"

She smiled then, the kind of smile that can melt any father's heart. And Joe knew that no matter how he felt about Sara, he was going to have to stay in Christmas just a little while longer.

BEFORE NIKKI EVEN GOT DRESSED that morning, she looked outside at the sky. Nothing but clouds. Not that there'd be stars in the morning.

But she didn't care. She perched next to the window and looked up into the swirling mass of white.

"I don't know if you can hear me, Mom, but I have to tell you thank-you. The first part of my wish has come true. Now if we can just get Dad to notice Sara..."

Chapter Eight

December 24, 9:00 a.m.

"Where are you going?" Joe asked his mother when a short while later she came down the stairs carrying the Mrs. Claus outfit.

"To town. The show must go on whether there's snow or not." She opened the hallway closet and pulled out her coat.

"Mom, we're in the middle of a blizzard. No one's going to come to a small-town craft show."

"It's not a craft show, it's a Victorian Christmas village. And we've advertised in all the papers. People are expecting us to put on a show." He could hear the hope in her voice, along with the uncertainty. "We might not get as much business as we had hoped, but the people will come."

"The ones who live in town anyway," he added a bit grimly.

"People are tough in this part of the country and they don't let a little snow keep them from celebrating Christmas," she stated with a confidence meant to convince herself, as well as him.

"You're the one who begged me not to leave in this weather," he reminded her.

She fixed him with a stare. "And your point is?"

"If I'm not going anywhere, then others aren't going to be, either. Mom, do you honestly think anyone is going to come to town today?"

"It doesn't matter whether they do or not—I still have to be there," she said, pulling on her coat. "We've worked weeks to get ready for this one day. If the only people who show up are the people living in town, then so be it. But we're not going to quit now. We're not quitters, Joe."

"No, you're too stubborn to quit," he said on a sigh of resignation.

Anxiety lined her face and clouded her eyes. "Maybe we should have."

He felt like the world's worst son. He draped an arm around her shoulder and said, "No, Mom, you shouldn't have. You're right. You can't quit now. I'm proud of all the effort you've put into making this day a success."

She gave him a kiss on the cheek. "Thanks for saying that. Now I need to get going."

"Do you have double duty? Cooking and playing Mrs. Claus?" he asked as she carefully zipped the red velvet dress into a garment bag.

"I'm just going to get things started in the kitchen at the Stable. Once the rest of the crew gets there, I'll head over to the North Pole with Nikki."

Joe frowned. "Nikki's going with you?"

"She's one of Santa's helpers—or had you forgotten?" She turned to holler up the stairs for her granddaughter. Within minutes Nikki came skipping down the steps. She was dressed in green from head to toe, her blond hair covered by a pointed cap that had bells on its tip that jingled with every step she took.

"How do I look?" she asked the two of them, posing on the bottom step.

Alice gave her a hug. "Too cute for words."

"Dad?" She looked at Joe, waiting for his comment.

"You look good, Nik." He tinkled the bells on her hat. "You sound good, too."

"Sara's going to help me put on makeup so my face is green, too. You don't care, do you?" The appeal in her eyes tugged at his heartstrings.

And then there was the look his mother gave him. It clearly said, "Don't rain on her parade."

Not that Joe would have. He could see what being an elf meant to his daughter. "No, I don't mind," he said with a smile.

She grinned back at him and gave him a hug. "Thanks." Then she reached for her jacket, which hung from the newel post. "Come on, Grandma. We'd better go or we'll be late."

"Maybe I should give you a ride," Joe offered. "It's snowing awfully hard."

"Don't worry," his mother answered. "Sara's picking us up."

"In what? I thought the front end was damaged on her mother's car."

"She has a loaner from Fritz." Just then a horn honked and Alice said, "I bet that's her now. Why don't you come have lunch with us around noon?"

"You can take a sleigh ride, Dad. It'll be really cool with the snow falling and everything," Nikki suggested.

"One sleigh ride is enough, thank you," he declared.

Nikki groaned and he quickly added, "But I will stop

in to see my elf in action." He tweaked the bell on her cap.

They quickly buttoned coats and pulled on boots, then with a wave were out the front door. "Don't forget to take care of Kris," Nikki called out as she hurried outside.

Joe watched them tread carefully across the snowy walk to the car. Sitting behind the wheel of a big old blue Pontiac was Sara, her hair a mass of curls that dangled about her face. He felt a familiar stirring inside him. He knew she smelled like some tropical flower— that's what he remembered from nuzzling his face in the silky tresses.

He thought about how good it had felt to have her in his arms at the cabin. Sweet. And hot. And exciting. Just thinking about it made him ache with desire. It had been a long time since a woman had been able to arouse him so easily. What was it about first love that kept it so tempting?

He knew his mistake had been in kissing her. If he hadn't touched her, he wouldn't be fantasizing about what it would be like to finish what they had started at the cabin.

Even long after the Pontiac had disappeared down the street, he could picture her lying in front of that fireplace, her lips swollen from his kisses, her skin so soft to his touch. It was an image he had difficulty pushing out of his mind.

A distraction was what he needed. A physical distraction. He pulled on his jacket, boots and stocking cap and went outside to shovel his mother's walk. It didn't matter that the snow was falling as fast as he could clear it away; he just kept shoveling.

He saw a couple of his mother's neighbors walking

toward Main Street—on their way to the celebration, no doubt. They waved and asked him how he was. He lied and said, ''Good.''

Frustrated would have been an honest answer. And not just because he couldn't get home to California for Christmas. Seeing the joy on Nikki's face upon hearing they were going to stay had tempered his disappointment at not being able to leave. No, his frustration was due to one blue-eyed blonde who had managed to get under his skin like no woman had ever been able to do. No matter how hard he tried, he couldn't stop thinking about Sara...and what had happened at the cabin. Or what might have happened had Frank Feester not shown up when he did.

It was such thoughts that tempted him to walk into town to see her. But then what good would it do? She was immersed in making the Victorian Christmas celebration happen. And even if she weren't, every time they were together they ended up arguing. So he resisted the temptation to go find her.

What he couldn't resist, however, was walking to the end of the block to see how much action was taking place in town. Just as he expected, there was no steady stream of traffic. Actually there was no traffic. Colored lights glowed along the shop fronts, Buzz's sleigh sat parked on Main Street, but the only activity anywhere was a boy shoveling the sidewalk and two men trying to push a car that was stuck in a driveway.

Joe heaved a long sigh and shook his head. Why hadn't Sara listened to him? Even if the snowstorm hadn't struck, chances were slim that their Christmas village would attract enough people to raise any significant money. Not on Christmas Eve.

He decided to go back inside and get a warm cup of

coffee. As he shoved his gloves into his pocket, he found the knit headband. Sara's headband. The one she wanted returned. It was all the motivation he needed to walk into town.

He stopped at each of the shops converted into attractions. The only bodies in the North Pole were Mr. and Mrs. Claus, Nikki and a handful of locals. In Mother Goose Land there were several small children— all belonging to mothers working at the Christmas celebration. The old hardware store boasted tables filled with crafts, but only a couple of familiar faces admired the handiwork. At each of the places Joe asked the same question. "How's business?"

And at every place he got the same answer. "It's been a little slow." Which Joe knew meant that only the people who lived in town had braved the snow. Not that he could blame anyone for not wanting to be out on a such a day.

He could barely see in front of him as the snow swirled in his face. He pulled open the door to the Stable, grateful to be out of the cold. When he walked in, the first thing he heard was a record on the jukebox playing "I Saw Mommy Kissing Santa Claus." It was all he heard. No rattle of dishes and cutlery, no chatter of voices. Three women wearing aprons over their dresses sat at a table. One rose as he entered.

"Welcome to Christmas. Would you care for something to eat or drink?" she asked, coming over to greet him. Joe saw that she wore a name tag that said Midge.

"Actually I'm here to see Sara Richards, Midge. Is she here?" He glanced around the bar but didn't see her.

Recognition dawned in the woman's eyes. "Oh! You're Alice's son, Joe, aren't you? We heard you were back. I should have recognized you. You really haven't changed a bit," she said with a little laugh. "Come on in. Sara's in the back. I'll get her for you."

Joe held up his hand. "No, it's all right. I'll find her." He walked through the swinging doors into the kitchen, where two older woman stood icing cookies. Like Midge, they fussed over his identity, wishing him a merry Christmas before he went to find Sara in the storage room.

She stood in front of a small mirror hanging on the wall. She wore a dark blue velvet dress with a full skirt that fell to the floor. The style emphasized the fullness of her breasts and the slimness of her waist and made her looked exactly like what Joe thought a Victorian lady would look. In her hand was an embroidered hand-kerchief. One look at her splotchy face told him she had needed it. She'd been crying.

When she noticed his reflection behind her in the mirror, she turned around and asked, "Did you come to gloat?"

"No. I came to return this." He handed her the head-band.

She took it from him and sniffled. "Thanks." When he didn't leave right away, she said, "You can go now."

"You shouldn't turn away a paying customer," he said lightly.

"If you want to order food, you'll have to go out front," she said between sniffles.

"I thought maybe you'd keep me company. Isn't that your role? To be the hostess?"

"You'll have to forgive me if I'm not quite in the mood to be the proper Victorian lady just now." She lifted her hooped skirt in order that she could step around him.

"You don't have to put on your bonnet and gloves. I won't tell anyone," he teased. When she didn't even crack a hint of a smile, he said, "I'm sorry about the snowstorm."

"I'm sure you are. You'll have to stay here for Christmas with all of us boring, narrow-minded people." She shoved her handkerchief into her pocket and stiffened her shoulders as if bracing to do battle with him.

"No, that's not why I'm sorry. The snow means all of your hard work will have been for nothing. Just because I was opposed to the idea doesn't mean I wanted to see you fail, Sara."

"Well, I'm going to fail. We haven't even had one person outside of Christmas come into any of the shops." Her voice broke and she looked down at her hands. Just when he thought the tears might fall, she said, "I should have known better. I'm not a stupid person."

"No, you're not. If anyone is, I'd say it's the people who forecast the weather. They didn't predict this storm and you certainly had no way of knowing what the weather conditions would be. This isn't your fault, Sara."

She looked up at him, eyes brimming with unshed tears. "If it's not my fault, then why do I feel like such a loser?"

"You're not a loser," he said gently but firmly.

"Yes, I am." She hiccuped again. "Everyone in town was counting on me and I let them down." Then a solitary tear trickled down her cheek and her lips began to quiver.

He couldn't resist. He pulled her into his arms and comforted her, allowing her to sob into his shoulder. "Don't cry, Sara. It's not the end of the world."

"No, just the end of C-Christmas," she said on a sob.

"No, it's not. Everything will work out," he said softly, brushing his hands across the blond curls, inhaling their tropical fragrance.

He held her in his arms, letting her vent all her frustration. For the first time since he'd been back he saw a Sara who wasn't self-confident. Instead she was vulnerable, needing his understanding and compassion. It was a Sara he found even more attractive than the fire-spitting antagonist who usually confronted him.

As he held her in his arms, it seemed the most natural thing in the world to smooth her hair, to place tiny kisses on her forehead. What began as a gesture of comfort, however, quickly changed to something else. Partly because she moved against him in a suggestive caress, but mainly because he couldn't resist planting little kisses across her cheek in a warm trail that led to her mouth. Once he felt her soft lips beneath his, the whisper-light contact turned into a hungry caress that sent an explosion of desire through him.

Her lips parted, allowing his tongue to move into her mouth, fueling the fire of longing that threatened to make him forget everything except her. Just as had happened at the cabin, she clung to him, matching his passion, returning his kisses as if she wanted them to go on forever.

Joe needed more than kisses. He wanted to feel her, all of her. To run his hands across breasts pushed close to his chest. For a moment he forgot they were in the back room of a bar, and his fingers reached for the button on her bodice. Before they could find their way inside the dress, however, he heard a voice.

"Um…Sara…um…I'm sorry, but there's a busload of people getting off right in front of the Stable." Midge was in the doorway.

Joe wasn't sure the look of bewilderment on Sara's face had been caused by the arrival of tourists or the fact that they had been so hot for each other they could have easily torn off each other's clothes.

"I'll be right there," she managed to say, her face turning a deep red as she realized that the young woman had witnessed their kissing.

"I think they want to eat," Midge added weakly.

"Good. We've got food," Sara answered, straightening the bodice of her dress. As soon as Midge was gone, she looked at Joe and said, "Now look what you've done. If it wasn't bad enough that Frank Feester caught us with our pants off, now Midge sees this!"

He wanted to ask her what *this* was, but she stomped away.

Joe followed her. "You wanted me to kiss you."

"No, I didn't."

"Liar."

As they burst into the kitchen, several pair of eyes were on them. Joe could only guess at what was going through Sara's head. Gone was the vulnerability that had allowed him to pull her into his arms. She was full of determination, taking charge of the situation at hand.

"Sara, I think we'd better talk," he said, placing a hand on her arm before she could step into the bar.

"Later. I need to see to the guests," she said, shaking her arm away from his.

It annoyed Joe that she could so easily put what had happened between them on the back burner. For the second time since he'd been home, passion had flared between them, and again it had been doused by the arrival of another person. It made him wonder what would happen if he and Sara were alone without the possibility of any interruptions.

"The guests can wait," Joe tried to tell her, but as they stepped into the bar he saw the reason Midge had come to get Sara. To Joe's amazement, people had filled several of the tables. Through the glass windows he saw a bus parked out front.

"There are twelve of them," Midge said in a low voice to Sara. "They're Japanese."

"I can see that," Sara returned in an equally low voice.

"Apparently they were on the way back from a casino up north."

"They must have seen our ads," Sara said, grabbing menus from the end of the bar.

Joe spoke up. "The driver probably got tired of battling the poor conditions and decided to pull off the road."

Sara gave Joe a cross look, then went to greet the guests. It didn't take long for her to learn the reason they were in town. They were stranded. Not that it mattered to Sara. She and her crew went to work, happy to provide them with a meal.

Joe went out to the bus where the driver was trying to radio his location to company headquarters.

"It's pretty bad out there, eh?" Joe asked, perching himself on the bus steps.

"Treacherous. The sheriff told us they're probably going to close the highway before long. I don't suppose this town has a hotel?"

"No, no hotel."

"Well, I'm not taking this baby another block. We're lucky we made it this far. You should have seen the cars in the ditch."

"Come on inside. At least it's warm and dry," Joe said, urging the man to follow him back into the bar.

When he told Sara the highway was probably going to be closed and their guests wouldn't be able to get back on the bus, she said, "Then they'll have to stay here."

Seeing the bus parked out front brought Nikki to the Stable. "Grandma wants to know what's going on."

Joe explained that the Japanese tourists were stranded in Christmas. All of them found Nikki's elf costume amusing, giggling every time she moved and her hat tinkled. Nikki wasted no time in making friends with them and in discovering that all but two of them had found the perfect souvenir in Minnesota—a stuffed animal in the shape of a blue ox.

"They liked the legend of Paul Bunyan," Nikki explained to her father.

"Too bad it's winter. They'd enjoy the amusement park not far from here," Sara commented. "Everything is jumbo size—just like Paul Bunyan. There's even a big blue ox outside the gates."

"That sounds awesome!" Nikki's widened in anticipation. "Maybe we can come back in the summer and I can go there, huh, Dad?"

"Maybe," Joe said noncommittally.

Nikki's thoughts were too preoccupied with the stranded travelers to press the issue, much to Joe's relief.

"Where is everyone going to sleep?" she asked.

It was Sara who answered, "I called the mayor. He's rounding up cots and blankets to put in the town hall."

"Maybe they want to shop at the craft fair before they go over there," Nikki suggested. "Two of them didn't get to buy a blue ox because the souvenir place ran out."

Sara smiled. "Then they should definitely visit the craft fair. I saw some adorable teddy bears over there. And they should go see Santa and Mrs. Claus, right?"

Nikki nodded eagerly. Before Joe knew it, the twelve Japanese tourists were filing out of the bar and following Nikki up the street to the North Pole. Sara turned her attention to helping the waitresses clear the tables.

"Can I talk to you for a minute?" Joe asked her. "In private."

She stopped what she was doing to look up at him. "Every eye in the place is on us, Joe," she said in a low voice meant only for his ears.

He knew she was right. No doubt Midge had told everyone working at the Stable just what it was that she had seen in the storage room.

"They're already talking about us." His voice was just as low as hers.

"If we go in the back room, it'll only make things worse," Sara warned him, casting a sideways glance at one of the waitresses.

"But we need to talk."

"Not now," she said through clenched teeth, then continued to pile dirty dishes into the large plastic dishpan. Before she could lift it, Joe pushed her aside and did it for her.

"I'll carry this into the kitchen," he told her, which didn't bring a smile of thanks.

"Why don't you go see if your mother needs help," she suggested coolly.

"If I'm going to help someone, I'm going to help you." He refused to take no for an answer.

"Very well." She marched into the kitchen, gestured for him to set the dishpan down, then handed him a pair of rubber gloves. "You can help me wash dishes."

It wasn't what Joe wanted to do, but he wouldn't give her the chance to find fault with his offer. He took off his jacket and tied an apron around his waist and dug into the task at hand.

Although Sara worked in the kitchen, too, it was impossible to talk privately since a couple of older women had manned the grill. When they decided to taste the pecan pie, taking their slices along with a cup of coffee out into the eating area of the bar, Joe breathed a sigh of relief.

Sara looked as if she wanted to escape with them, but he stopped her. "Wait. Please don't run away."

"I don't run away from anything in life, Joe."

"No? What about what happened after the prom?" She colored and he immediately wished he hadn't brought up the subject. That was ten years ago and what really concerned him was what had happened to them in the storage room. "I'm sorry. I shouldn't have said that. I don't like the fact that every time we're together we act as if we're facing off in a debate."

She faced him and said, "I don't like it, either. Apology accepted."

Joe felt as if they were finally making progress. "Sara, we can't pretend that what we did at the cabin didn't happen. We've kissed...actually we've done more than kiss."

"We shouldn't have. At the cabin I had been drinking and today...well, today I was upset and..."

"So are you saying you regret what happened?"

Before she could answer, Nikki burst through the swing doors. "Sara, guess what! There's a whole bunch of football players coming to eat! Eleven of them. I counted."

Sara looked at Joe. "I...the answer is no." Then she turned and headed for the bar. Joe removed the apron from around his waist and went after her. She had said no. That had to mean she didn't regret what had happened...but what exactly did it mean?

Nikki hadn't been wrong about the guests filing into the bar. They were men. Huge men with thick necks. And all looked hungry enough to finish off the rest of the food in the kitchen.

It turned out they were members of a professional football team that had gone to a lodge in the woods for a couple of days of snowmobiling. They had started for the cities early that morning, but with the poor visibility and driving conditions they hadn't gotten as far as they'd hoped. Now they were hungry.

They managed to put a significant dent in the food supply. Joe didn't like them being in the Stable, especially since several of them flirted shamelessly with Sara. Before they had even finished eating, he knew he wasn't going to be washing up after this crew. Before Sara could hand him the apron, he grabbed a shovel and went out front to clear the snow away from the walks. He hated being out in the cold, but it would have been more humiliating to be wearing an apron and rubber gloves while the jocks flirted with Sara.

Joe thought they were a cocky bunch. When Sara told them they wouldn't probably make it out of Christmas because of the weather, they dismissed her warning with coy smiles. That's why Joe grinned smugly when after lunch they visited the other shops, spent money for the cause, then piled back in the motor home in which they were traveling.

No sooner had they departed than a van arrived. Out jumped nine cheerleaders who had been at a basketball tournament and were on their way back home to a neighboring town less than fifty miles away.

Again Sara went to work feeding the girls, whose chaperone told the perky teens that no matter what the football players had decided, this group wasn't going to even try to make it home until the snow stopped.

Joe looked at Sara. "Now what? You got rid of the football players, but the Japanese guys have the town hall. Where are you going to put nine teenagers?"

"I can take a couple extra at my house," Midge piped up.

"Me, too," said one of the cooks.

"I don't have any extra beds, but I'll call to see if I can find someone who does," a third woman volunteered.

So while the cheerleaders ate turkey sandwiches, Sara and her helper made dozens of phone calls. They were able to place the remaining five girls with the minister and his wife, who, as it turned out, were alone this Christmas since both of their sons were overseas.

As soon as the arrangements had been made and the Stable was once again quiet, Nikki asked Sara, "Do you know that song 'The Twelve Days of Christmas'?"

"You mean the partridge in a pear tree?"

Nikki nodded exuberantly. "We might have our own twelve days in twelve hours. We've had twelve tourists, eleven football players, ten stuffed animals, nine cheerleaders," she rattled off on her fingers. "Now we need to have eight somebodies show up, then seven, then six, then five...."

Joe didn't want to dampen his daughter's enthusiasm, but he had to say, "I can't imagine anyone else being out in this weather."

"Some might not have heard the warnings, and the snowstorm did come up rather suddenly," Sara pointed out.

"And at this time of the year, everyone wants to be with their families," Midge added. "I wouldn't be surprised if we didn't get more. It's only three o'clock."

And before another hour had passed there were seven more unexpected guests. Nikki couldn't believe only seven carolers climbed out of the minivan when it pulled up outside the Stable. "Are you sure there isn't one more of you?" she asked the group of men and women who had been on their way to sing Christmas carols at a nursing home.

"No, just the seven of us," the leader of the group replied. "We'd be happy to sing for you folks."

So someone unplugged the jukebox and let the visitors sing while Sara and her crew prepared more food for their guests. Just when Joe thought it couldn't get any crazier than what it already was, Nikki raced to tell him of another vehicle that had turned off the highway.

"Dad, it's six lady wrestlers in a car. Get it? Six! That means five must be on the way." Her eyes sparkled with excitement.

Joe wondered what lady wrestlers would be doing in northern Minnesota. He soon found out that the university at Morris was one of the few colleges in the Midwest to have a women's wrestling team. The ladies were actually college students and a delight for Nikki. As soon as they had eaten, she took them to the North Pole, then over to Mother Goose Land.

They had barely gone out the door when a sport-utility vehicle brought five more people in from the storm. They were ice fishermen, wanting to take advantage of the barometric pressure before the storm hit.

By now everyone in town had heard about the stranded visitors—and the twelve hours of Christmas. Bets were being made as to whether four, three, two and one would show. It was already a foregone conclusion that eight had been skipped.

Just before sundown a small plane landed in Buzz Gustafson's field. Aboard were three nuns on their way to a religious retreat in northern Minnesota. Buzz brought them to town, one by one, on his tractor. By the time the last of the nuns was safely seated in the Stable, a car carrying four Santas arrived.

Once more Sara called to find beds for the additional stranded travelers. As Joe watched her at work, he realized that there was a reason why she had always championed so many lost causes. She had a big heart.

She also had an abundance of patience. There had been a steady stream of mouths to feed ever since the first busload of tourists had arrived. Now an eclectic assortment of guests sat in the Stable, eating, drinking and trying to be as merry as possible considering they were stranded in a strange town on Christmas Eve.

Although it was nearly impossible to navigate the streets of Christmas in an automobile, many of the locals came on snowmobiles to collect their house guests. Joe was surprised at the number of residents who chipped in to help. Many invited strangers to share in their Christmas celebrations. They opened their hearts and their doors in a way Joe hadn't expected to find anywhere, and especially not in Christmas.

When three hours passed without anyone stopping in the town, the consensus was that the twelve hours of

Christmas wouldn't present them with eight, two or one new arrivals. Then someone hollered into the Stable, "There's a pickup spun off on Highway 75. Dick Brewer saw it when he was out snowmobiling. He says there are two people in it."

Again Joe saw Nikki's eyes light up. "See? It's not over yet."

Joe watched as the snowmobile rescue team left in the near whiteout conditions to get the stranded motorists. All eyes in the Stable were on the door, watching and waiting.

Finally Nikki said, "They're here!"

They were a young married couple, Joel and Rita Davis, who had been on their way to the hospital in Alex. It only took one look at Rita to see why. She was going to have a baby and soon, Joe thought, judging by the expression on her face.

"Is there a doctor in town?" Joel asked anxiously as they helped Rita into the Stable.

"No, but Donna Raymond is a nurse," Midge told everyone. "I'll call her."

"Where am I going to have the baby?" the frightened Rita asked her husband, clinging to his coat sleeve as she looked around the bar anxiously.

Joe said, "What about upstairs? Didn't Chester used to have an apartment up there?"

"The building's been closed since he lost his liquor license and he moved back to the farm," Alice answered. "I doubt anything's up there."

"Does anyone have a key?"

"I do," Sara answered, pulling a large metal ring from her pocket. She jangled the keys in midair. "One of these must work. I'll go find out."

Joe was tempted to go with her, but he let Nikki be

the one who ran after Sara as she disappeared through the swing doors. While everyone else in the bar tried not to fuss over the fact that there was a woman who looked as if she might have a baby right there in their midst, Alice ordered the people around her to fetch clean towels, get ice chips, boil some water and a whole lot of other things. Joe wasn't sure exactly what was of significance. But one thing he had learned as a child was never to interrupt his mother when she was in her take-charge mode.

Everyone heaved a sigh of relief when Donna the nurse came stomping into the bar. Knowing it was an emergency and having been in the middle of her own family's holiday celebration, she hadn't taken the time to change but wore a green velvet dress with lace trim.

"Get her an apron!" someone hollered out.

"Better get her two," Alice added.

Fortunately for Rita Davis, Donna Raymond was not easily rattled. Twenty-three years of training showed itself as she calmly took charge of the situation.

More sighs of relief were heard when Sara reappeared and said, "There's a bed upstairs and there are clean linens."

Joel Davis scooped his wife into his arms and followed Sara to the apartment. Donna was at his side, muttering words of reassurance.

A silence settled on the Stable. They all went back to what they were doing, but hardly a word was uttered. It was as if they all waited for word of the birth.

"Is she gonna be okay, Dad?" Nikki asked. "She looked really scared."

It was Alice who answered her question. "She's in good hands. Donna's a good nurse. She's helped deliver many babies."

"This is so awesome," Nikki said on a note of wonder. "First we get the twelve hours of Christmas and now we get a couple having a baby with no place to go and they end up in a place called the Stable. It's like a miracle, isn't it, Grandma?"

Alice patted her hand. "Yes, it is, and isn't it wonderful that the two of you are here to be a part of it?" Her look encompassed both father and daughter.

Joe knew his mother expected Nikki to agree, but she wasn't expecting he would. "It's not exactly how we planned to spend Christmas, eh, Nik?" He gave his daughter's cap a tug, producing a jingle.

She giggled. "No. Are we even going to be able to get back to Grandma's or are we gonna have to sleep here on the floor?"

"Oh, we'll get back," Alice assured her.

"I hope Kris is okay." Nikki expressed concern over the animal.

Joe glanced at his watch. "I should probably go back and let her out. It's been a while since I left."

Alice patted his forearm. "You stay. I'll get Sam to walk me and Nikki home."

"We're not going to leave before the baby is born, are we?" Nikki wanted to know.

"Now, that depends on how long that baby takes to arrive," Alice answered.

"I hope it's soon." Nikki heaved a long sigh. "We need one baby to complete the twelve hours of Christmas."

"What about the eight spot? I thought we missed that one, too," Joe commented.

"We still have four hours to go. Eight more people could get stuck here," his daughter said optimistically.

Alice shuddered. "Let's hope not. I think Rita just took the last spare bed."

When Sara came through the swinging doors, another silence fell on the room as every head turned toward her expectantly. "Any action yet?" someone called out.

Sara shook her head. "Donna says it won't be long." She grabbed a bottle of soda from the bar and went back through the swing doors.

Joe wished he could have gone with her. Not because he wanted to be in the room when the baby was born. But because he wanted to be with Sara. When he had asked her if she had regretted nearly making love with him, she had said no. Certainly that had to mean that she had wanted it as much as he had?

At a quarter to midnight there was still no word of the baby's arrival. Joe could see that Nikki was about to fall asleep against her grandmother's shoulder. He pulled her onto his lap and cradled her in his arms.

"Maybe I should take you home," he murmured as he held her close.

"Uh-uh. Just let me stay until midnight. Please? I know the baby's going to come. She has to. It'll make our twelve hours of Christmas complete."

Joe didn't bother to remind her that they had missed the number eight. He couldn't. She was so caught up in the emotional scene that had unfolded in the Stable.

The room was so quiet Joe thought he could have heard a pin drop. All eyes were on the swinging doors through which Sara had disappeared, anticipating her return and the news she would bring.

As the hands on the clock slowly moved toward midnight, Joe could see the concern in everyone's eyes. "I sure hope everything is okay," someone remarked in a low voice that had everyone murmuring in agreement.

"Wouldn't it be neat if it were a boy?" One of the waitresses tried to break the tension with a positive question.

At two minutes to midnight Joe looked down and saw that Nikki had fallen asleep. He turned to his mother and asked, "Do you think I should take her home?"

"She'll be disappointed if you do."

Joe nodded.

A silence fell over the room once again as the hands of the clock slowly moved toward midnight. When they had passed the number twelve, several sighs could be heard. Then Sara came through the swinging doors.

A collective gasp of anticipation filled the room. Joe nudged Nikki's shoulder. "Wake up, Nik. Sara's back."

She came awake and asked, "Is it a partridge in a pear tree, Sara?"

Sara smiled. "No, it's much better. It's a little girl. Mary Catherine Davis."

Whoops of delight echoed throughout the bar.

"And she arrived exactly at midnight."

Applause welcomed the announcement. When everyone had finished cheering the news, Nikki told Sara, "It's just like another Christmas song. 'It Came Upon a Midnight Clear'."

"Only it's not exactly clear in Christmas, is it?" someone called out.

"When can I see her?" Nikki asked excitedly.

Joe reined his daughter into his arms once more. "There'll be plenty of time for that tomorrow."

Others in the Stable had similar thoughts. They straightened their chairs and reached for their coats. Midge said to Sara, "If everything's okay, we thought we'd leave, too, Sara," speaking on behalf of the kitchen crew.

"Everything looks good," she said with a grateful smile for the women who had worked so hard and so long to feed the stranded travelers. "You did a fantastic job today. Thank you for your help. All of you."

"I wouldn't have missed it for the world," Midge said, her sentiments quickly echoed by the others.

"I'm just sorry you had to miss spending Christmas Eve with your families. I never thought when we planned this celebration that we'd be here this late," Sara apologized.

All of them dismissed her concern. "There's always tomorrow. At least we can go home tonight. Look at how many are stranded here and having to spend Christmas in a strange bed away from their loved ones."

"Well, thank you. Everyone. Now I'd better go see how mother and daughter are doing." Once again she slipped through the swinging doors.

"Well, that's that. Nikki, you got your wish," Alice noted. "Now it's time for us to head home. Are you coming, Joe?"

He should go home. It would be the wise thing to do. The safe thing to do. But then he reminded himself. When had he ever played it safe when it came to Sara?

"You go on ahead. I have something I need to do first."

December 25, 12:40 a.m.

BY THE TIME SARA CAME back downstairs, everyone had gone home. To her surprise everything had been put away. All the chairs were turned upside down on the tables, the kitchen looked as clean as a whistle and not a thing was out of place.

The light was on in the kitchen, but the bar sat in darkness except for the neon glow of a small beer sign on the wall. She peeked her head through the swinging doors, and her breath caught in her throat.

On the bar were two candles. Tall red tapers set in tin cans. Between them was a bottle of strawberry wine.

Her heart began to race. She swallowed with difficulty, then said, "Joe?"

He didn't answer but instead let a record on the jukebox be his reply. "I'll Be Home for Christmas" filled the room.

Out of the darkness he walked toward her. "I'm here, Sara." He slid his arm through the swinging door and reached for her hand. "I think it's time I wish you a proper merry Christmas, don't you?"

Chapter Nine

The minute Joe's fingers met hers, her body began to tingle. He pulled her into the candlelit bar, the look in his eyes causing Sara to go weak at the knees. Each time she saw him, he seemed to become more attractive to her.

"I thought you'd be gone by now," she said, unsure what else there was to say to him.

"I think after everything that's happened, we deserve to have a little Christmas cheer." He led her over to the bar, where he pulled out a stool for her, then placed his hands on her waist and guided her to sit on it.

"Thank you," she said in a voice that to her own ears sounded weak. It was no wonder. Every time he touched her, she trembled inside. Not out of fear, but excitement. The look on his face reminded her that only hours earlier those hands that now nudged her waist had cupped her breasts. The memory created a longing in Sara that nearly had her sighing.

He took the stool beside her, his thigh rubbing up against hers as he moved closer to her. It was an intimacy she wanted, and she was pretty certain that he knew it, too.

"It's late. You should be home with Nikki celebrating Christmas," she said, her voice coming out almost as a whisper.

"I want to be here with you."

That caused her heart to skip a beat and her mouth to feel dry.

He reached for the bottle of strawberry wine.

"Where did you get that?" she asked with a half grin. "There hasn't been any liquor in this town since Chester lost his liquor license."

A furtive twinkle lit his eyes as he said, "Fortunately when Chester closed the place, he forgot that a certain teenager had worked for him. One who knew all the nooks and crannies of this place and secret hiding places."

"Gee, you really were a bad boy, weren't you?" she teased.

He grinned devilishly, wiggling his eyebrows as he poured them each a glass. "Yes, and it's a good thing I was. After what happened today, we both could use something a little stronger than eggnog."

She took a sip and wrinkled her nose. "Oooh. It's so sweet. Did we really like this stuff when we were kids?"

His eyes held hers. "Maybe we liked it because we weren't supposed to have it."

She knew he wasn't simply talking about the wine. "Maybe. Sometimes attraction can simply be explained as wanting the forbidden."

"There's nothing forbidden about our relationship now, is there, Sara?"

"Nothing I can think of," she answered candidly.

"Good." He filled first her glass, then his own with the wine.

She could feel his thigh pressing against hers and she

could smell the musky scent of his cologne. Never had she been more aware of him as a man than she was at that moment.

But then how could she not be when only earlier that day he had kissed her until she thought she would explode with longing for him? She had to look away from him, so great was the attraction she felt. She couldn't let him see it in her face.

"This snowstorm wasn't supposed to hit us. It was supposed to go north of here," she said, her fingers toying with the glass in her hands.

"Mom said she heard on the radio that they're calling it the storm of the century."

"It certainly will be one that this town remembers," she said on a sigh. "We practically doubled the population for the night."

"Those people are lucky to be stranded here."

That brought her head up with a jerk. "Lucky? Watch it, Joe. That almost sounded as if you don't think everyone is this town is narrow-minded and nosy."

"I don't think that."

She quirked an eyebrow. "You had me fooled."

"A man can change his opinion, can't he?"

"Did that happen?"

"Yes. The way people opened their doors to total strangers...well, it was one of those times when one's faith in humanity is revived. I never expected to see so much compassion and trust in people who were pulled away from their holiday celebrations to help people who really shouldn't have been on the road."

"So it's not such a bad town, after all? Is that what you're saying?"

"No, it's not," he said, trying to hold back his smile.

"Don't go falling off your stool in shock now that I've admitted that."

"It's nice to hear you say that," she said sincerely. "And I guess if you can make such an admission, I should be able to admit that I was wrong about the Victorian Christmas celebration. Even if we would have had a perfect day weather-wise, it probably wasn't the best way to save the town."

He reached across to gently touch her cheek with his finger. It was a simple gesture, but one that sent chills tingling through her. "Your heart was in the right place, Sara," he said huskily.

"Yes, well, unfortunately it didn't net us the money we needed to save the town," she reminded him, trying not to let him see the effect his touch had had on her breathing.

"Is the money that important?"

She looked at him in disbelief. "Of course it's important. We're going to lose our incorporation."

"But, Sara, having a mayor and an official spot on the map isn't what makes this town a good place to live. Today made me realize that," he told her, his eyes full of a compassion she hadn't seen in them before. "What makes this town special is the generosity of spirit and the trust you have in each other. You won't lose that with a piece of paper."

"But it isn't just a piece of paper, Joe. It's like a declaration of independence. It's a right to be who we are without someone else telling us what to do."

"We? You sound as if you consider this your home."

"It is still home to me. This town has good people, and I'd hate to see them lose the one thing that makes them all want to help each other out—concern for one another. That's a sentiment that seems to be becoming scarce.''

He nodded in understanding. ''People are cocooning, keeping to themselves.''

''Exactly.''

''Which is what makes what happened here today so extraordinary.''

''It didn't seem out of the ordinary to me. I was born and raised here and throughout my life I saw the same acts of kindness. You must have seen some of it, Joe.''

He shook his head. ''I don't know. Maybe I just wasn't looking for it.''

''Or maybe you didn't get to spend enough time here to see that happen.''

He shrugged. ''You could be right.''

For the first time since he had arrived, he didn't have the chip on his shoulder and she discovered that she liked the agreeable Joe as much as she liked the debating Joe. ''Do you realize that we've been sitting here talking and we haven't argued once?''

''As tired as I am, I doubt I have any fight left in me,'' he confessed.

''Whatever the reason, I think we should have a toast.'' She lifted her glass and said, ''To us, Joe.''

''To us,'' he echoed, a gleam in his eye that sent ripples of pleasure through her. When they had each taken a sip and set their glasses back down, he asked, ''Is there an us, Sara?''

She could see the time had come to discuss what had happened in the storeroom. And at the cabin. He wasn't going to let her evade the subject any longer.

''I think we can be friends, Joe.''

''Friends?''

"Yes. We don't need to snipe at each other constantly. Today proved that."

"And what about being more than friends?"

She could feel her body warm, and it wasn't because of the wine. For someone who had spent the past nine years in a cosmopolitan setting, she suddenly felt very small-town. She wished she had a one-liner ready to toss back at him to make it sound as if there were nothing unusual about the kisses they had shared, but she had never been good at flirting. Still wasn't.

She couldn't think of a single coy reply. Maybe because what she had felt when she was in his arms wasn't something easily put into words. Kissing Joe Gibson had been a revelation. It had shown her that she still had feelings for him, and to reduce those feelings to a flirtatious experience was something she didn't want to do. Something she couldn't do.

"I think there's a possibility that could happen," she said carefully. "I mean, I normally don't kiss my friends quite so intimately," she finally managed to say, keeping her eyes on her glass.

He placed a finger under her chin and forced her to look at him. "I'd like to think you don't kiss anyone like that but me."

There was a hope in his eyes, the same one she had seen ten years ago when he had asked her the same question. It would have been so easy for her to squash that hope with a negative answer. But she couldn't.

"I don't. I've never met anyone who could make me feel the way you do, Joe. It was special for me. Was it for you?" She felt her breath catch in her throat as she waited for his answer.

"You've always been special to me, Sara," he said huskily. She expected him to kiss her, but he didn't. His hand fell away from her chin and reached for his glass as he straightened away from her. "I never expected when I came back here that I'd want to spend every minute of my time with a woman."

"Is that what you want to do?"

"Yes."

They didn't talk or touch, but simply sat in silence, the only sound in the room the mechanism on the jukebox as it changed records.

"Then you're not still angry at me for keeping you from returning to California for Christmas?" she dared to ask.

"No. You did it because your heart is in the right place, Sara."

"You think so?"

"I know so." He reached out to place his palm across her breast. "I can feel it beating." Then his fingers moved and she trembled. He took the glass from her fingers and set it on the bar, then took her hands in his. "Dance with me." He slid off the bar stool, pulling her with him and into his arms.

On the narrow strip of tile next to the bar, they moved in rhythm to Elvis singing "Blue Christmas." Slow and easy, barely moving their feet, yet swaying to the rhythm. Memories rushed back, of that night when they had danced to the songs on the jukebox. Back then it had been nearly all country western and fifties and sixties rock-and-roll music.

They had only played the slow songs, clinging to each other like a pair of lovers who couldn't bear not to have as much of their bodies touching as possible. It had been the sexiest dancing Sara had ever done and, combined with the wine, had only fueled her desire for Joe.

"Do you remember what song we danced to over and over that night?" Joe asked, as if he could read her mind.

"'Crazy,' by Patsy Cline," she answered wistfully. "You told me you hated country western but you kept singing that song in my ear."

"Because I *was* crazy that night," he admitted.

"Maybe we both were," she suggested, hoping that didn't mean he regretted what had happened between them.

"It was a good kind of crazy," he said pulling her closer to him and erasing her doubts.

She melted into his arms, loving the strength she found there, the way he held her so tenderly as if she were the most precious thing in the world to him. With her breasts pressed close to his chest, they moved as one, just as they had ten years ago.

"You always were a good dancer," he said close to her ear.

"I think we're the right height for this," she told him, remembering that ten years ago he had said that they had fit together perfectly—another sign of how they were meant to be together. Never once had he stepped on her toes or bumped her knees. They had been in sync, their minds and their bodies.

And now as they swayed to the slow Christmas song, she felt the same way. "I'm glad you're home for Christmas, Joe," she said softly.

He lifted his head. "You really mean that?"

She nodded, her heart racing at the look that was in his eyes. He wanted to kiss her. They both knew it, and there was no point in denying it because she wanted the same thing.

Boldly she reached up to cover his mouth with hers.

She wanted it to be a sweet kiss, the kind of kiss that a woman gave a man when she wanted to wish him a merry Christmas. But just as it had happened the other two times they had kissed, passion flared between them.

Soon they were no longer moving to the rhythm of the music, but moving to another rhythm. That of their bodies clinging to each other, trying to get even closer as their mouths hungrily devoured each other's. Sara felt the familiar longing echo through her. A small whimper escaped as once more his hands found the most sensitive areas of her flesh.

But like the other times they had been in each other's arms, before they could proceed to the next level of intimacy, they were interrupted. This time it wasn't a person, but the jukebox. A record jammed causing a horrible screeching sound that had both of them pulling back and grimacing.

"I see Chester never had this thing fixed," Joe said as he hurried over to the jukebox and rapped on it with his palm. The record fell into place and strains of "Silent Night" filled the room. But the moment had been interrupted.

"Things really haven't changed, have they?" he said with a reflective grin as he walked back toward her.

It was enough of a distraction for Sara to realize that the last thing she wanted to do was make love in a bar. Not that she didn't want Joe. She did, but not on Christmas Eve in the back room of the Stable.

"I should probably get going home. It's late," she said reluctantly.

"There's more wine left in the bottle, more songs on the jukebox," he tried to tempt her.

"One glass is enough tonight."

"You sure?"

It was so tempting to say no, but she nodded all the same. As she pulled on her coat, the phone rang. Joe answered it. She only heard his end of the conversation, but it was enough to tell her that it was his mother who had called.

"Is anything wrong?" Sara asked when he had hung up.

"I'm needed," he said reaching for his jacket. "Actually a vet is needed, but Mom says she can't get one to come out in the snow."

"Kris is having her babies?" Sara asked.

"Want to come see?"

"I wouldn't miss it."

EVEN THOUGH IT WAS nearly two o'clock in the morning, the Christmas lights still lit the Gibson home. Alice, watching out the window for Joe, had the door opened before he had even climbed the porch steps.

"Sara, come on in." The smile on his mother's face told him the welcome wasn't for him, but for his companion. To Joe she said, "I'm glad you're home. I'm not sure what I should do."

"Nikki's not up, is she?" he asked, shrugging out of his jacket.

"She wanted to stay up, but she fell asleep on my bed. Not that I blame her. I don't know how much longer I can make it, either," she told them.

"You go to bed, Mom. I'll take care of Kris," Joe insisted, giving her a gentle nudge toward the stairs. "Where is she?"

"Oh, she's in your room," she said. "You will call me if you need any help, won't you?"

"Yes, Mom, we will," Joe assured her. Then he

turned to Sara. "Have you ever had a dog give birth before?"

Sara nodded. "Several times. They're pretty self-sufficient."

"I was hoping you'd say that." He led her to his room on the second floor. When his mother had said Kris was in his room, he hadn't expected that she'd be in his bed.

"Oh, my. She's picked a good spot, hasn't she?" Sara said with a wry grin.

"I don't suppose we should try to move her," Joe remarked.

"I think it's too late. Looks like the firstborn is about to arrive."

Joe huddled close to Sara, his arm around her as they watched the miraculous delivery of Kris's puppies. Having her at his side made the scene unfolding even more poignant for Joe, as they marveled over the wonders of nature.

"Looks like she's doing just fine," Sara said softly when he expressed concern for the dog.

"How many more is she going to have, do you think?" Joe wondered.

"Nikki would be delighted if it were eight. They may have come after midnight, but it's still Christmas," Sara noted.

"You forget. The eleven football players left," Joe reminded her.

"Oh—didn't you hear? They're back," she told him. "They didn't get very far before they turned around and headed back to town. Luckily they have a motor home, which they parked at Buzz Gustafson's place. At least we didn't need to go find more beds."

Joe thought it was a good place for them. He wanted them as far away from Sara as possible.

To Sara and Joe's amazement, by the time Kris had finished her labor, there were eight puppies. Six were black, two were brown-and-black mixes.

"Looks like the father might have been a black Lab," Sara noted. "I may be an aunt. Our dog, Royal, is a black Lab."

"I have to go wake up Nikki. She's going to go nuts when she sees this," Joe said, giving Sara's arm a squeeze before he left.

As he expected, his daughter was ecstatic to see the eight puppies. So was his mother, who wasn't too tired after all to get up and take a peek at the newborns.

"They look like they don't have any eyes," Nikki said, watching as the tiny pups nestled close to their mother.

"They're just not open yet," Sara told her.

"They're so tiny…and so cute. I wish we could take one home with us," Nikki crooned sympathetically.

"They're too small to take away from Kris just yet," Joe told her.

"Maybe once they're weaned you can take one," Alice suggested, which produced a frown on Joe's face.

Seeing his reaction, Nikki did her best to convince him to change his mind. "Ralph is getting old. We're going to need to think about getting a new dog sooner or later."

"I'll think about it," Joe said cautiously, which produced a whoop of delight from his daughter.

Joe didn't miss the way she cuddled up close to Sara. It was easy to see why Nikki had become so fond of Sara in such a short time. She had so much patience, explaining the process of birth to a nine-year-old. But then Sara had always been like that with everyone. Patient, kind, tolerant. He was the only one she ever seemed to get edgy with.

"Dad, where are you going to sleep? She made a mess of your bed," Nikki pointed out.

"Nikki, you can climb in with Grandma and let your dad have the roll-away," Joe heard his mother say.

"Ma, you don't have to do that. I can sleep on the couch downstairs," he told her.

"I'd offer you a bed at our house, but the spare room has lady wrestlers in it," Sara said with a grin.

"I'm sure I'll be fine on the couch."

"You'll get a crick in your neck. You're too tall for the couch," Alice warned him. "I'll sleep there and you can take my bed."

"Ma, I'm not taking your bed."

"Yes, you are."

"No, I'm not. And I don't want to hear another word about it," he stated emphatically.

As soon as it was determined that Kris had finished giving birth and the puppies were going to be all right, Joe insisted that Nikki go to bed. Alice offered to make coffee for Sara.

"You and Joe can have a cup while I get Nikki to bed. You can sit down in front of the fire and no one will disturb you," his mother suggested.

"Thanks, Alice, but I really should get home," Sara answered with a gentle smile.

"I'll walk you back," Joe offered, pleased that he would have some time to talk to Sara alone. He whisked Sara out of the house before his mother had a chance to say another word. What he didn't need was for his mother to be playing matchmaker again.

Once they were outdoors he said to Sara, "Why is it

that I feel as if I'm fifteen years old when I'm back home?"

She chuckled. "The same reason I do, I guess. I think it's hard for a parent to stop parenting, no matter how old their children are."

"That doesn't mean *I* have to revert to juvenile behavior. I'm sorry about what happened back there at the house. It was like a scene out of a sitcom."

Sara giggled. "It wasn't that bad. Besides, your mother's a dear."

"She's very fond of you. So is Nikki."

"You've done a good job with her, Joe. It can't be easy raising a daughter alone."

"I've had a lot of support from my in-laws. They all live in California."

They talked about their families until they reached the Richards home. Then Joe said, "Do you need help with anything tomorrow? Cleaning up? Getting the stranded travelers fed?"

She groaned. "I hadn't thought about breakfast. I suppose we'll have to open the Stable in the morning— at least for the people sleeping at the town hall. There isn't a café in town anymore."

"Tell me what time and I'll be there," he offered.

"It's Christmas Day, Joe. You need to be with your daughter."

The possibility that the football players might be the ones sitting in the Stable had Joe saying, "That doesn't mean we can't show up at the Stable in the morning and help feed everybody breakfast."

"I'll find someone to help in the morning," she assured him. "Your mom's having company for dinner."

"And where will you be tomorrow?"

"I hope with my family—provided the roads get plowed and my sister and brother can get here."

"Will I get a chance to wish you a merry Christmas tomorrow, or do I have to do that tonight?"

"Why don't you stop over after you've had dinner? Dad usually has some Christmas cheer in the house."

"I'd like that."

"Me, too."

They had reached the front porch and stood at the door. He realized that saying good-night was not something he wanted to do. If they weren't in Christmas, he would have asked her to spend the night at his home.

But they were in Christmas. Standing on a porch in the cold. He wanted to kiss her, to cover her mouth with his and not stop kissing her until the ache inside him went away. Only he knew that wouldn't happen, not tonight.

He simply lifted her hands in his and said, "Several times we've started something that we haven't been able to finish because of tow trucks, stranded travelers or a jukebox."

"I'm not sure I know what you mean by *finish*, Joe," she said, her breath coming out in a little white cloud in the cold night air.

"I think you do, Sara," he said, holding her gaze.

"Finishing brings complications," she said quietly.

"I've never known you to run away from a challenge." He squeezed her hands, then placed a butterfly kiss on her cheek. "Good night."

He would have walked away, but she kept hold of his hands. Before he knew it, she was kissing him, boldly, passionately. He forgot about the cold, forgot that they were on the front porch in front of her parents' house.

Then the porch light went on and the door opened. Startled, they pushed each other away.

"Oh, it's you, Sara. I'm sorry." There at the door in his pajamas was her father.

"It's all right, Dad. I was just coming in," she told him.

"No hurry," he said, clearing his throat in embarrassment. "Good seeing you, Joe," he added before closing the door again.

Sara giggled. "What were you saying about feeling fifteen again?"

He smiled. "I'd better go." He gave her hand a gentle squeeze, then walked away. All the way home he found himself humming "I'll Be Home for Christmas."

Chapter Ten

Although the snow had stopped somewhere around midnight, the winds had continued to howl during the wee hours of the morning, creating blizzard conditions that made it impossible for snowplows to clear the roads. Any hopes that the stranded travelers would be able to get back on the road bright and early on Christmas morning were dashed with the news report that Highway 75 would remain closed until after noon.

Just as they had the previous evening, the residents of Christmas made room for the additional guests, feeding them breakfast and inviting them into their homes to share in their holiday celebrations. It wasn't only the travelers whose plans had been interrupted. With virtually no movement on the roads, many families spent the day away from loved ones. Sara's sister and brother-in-law couldn't get to town for dinner, nor could her aunts and uncles. Chairs that would have normally been occupied by family members held strangers who marveled at the generous spirit of their hosts.

Despite what Joe had said to Sara about a piece of paper not being able to destroy the meaning of what made the town special, she knew that unless a miracle happened, in seven days Christmas would lose its autonomy. Although the miracles that had happened last night dulled the pain of the failure of their Victorian Christmas celebration, the truth was the town was going to dissolve into Denville unless a bigger miracle occurred.

The storm had dumped over a foot of snow on the region, then moved eastward, leaving a sparkling display of glistening wires and tree limbs in its aftermath. Every time Sara glanced out the window, she saw a winter wonderland that made her thankful she had come home for the holidays. With everything that was going on around her, she appreciated the new layer of snow. It was as if nature was saying that there would be a new beginning for their town, too.

A few four-wheel-drive vehicles managed to move across town, but mainly folks trudged through the snow to get to church or to visit one another. The only sound to be heard was the occasional roar of a snowmobile or a snowblower along with the screeches of pleasure of the children playing.

Thanks to the generosity of the people in town, Sara didn't have to feed anyone at the Stable on Christmas morning. She spent most of the day with her parents—and the lady wrestlers, who she discovered were excellent cooks and insisted on helping Sara's mother prepare dinner.

When word came that the plows had finally cleared the roads, she hurried over to tell the Davises. Before they said goodbye to Sara, they thanked her for all of her help and for giving Mary Catherine the red sleeper with a tiny Christmas tree embroidered on the front. Sara had found it in the craft fair and had wanted the new parents to have it for their daughter. Earlier that day many of the residents had dropped off baby items, including disposable diapers, baby wipes and blankets.

Word quickly spread that the highway was open, resulting in a flurry of activity in the small town. Pickups sporting plows on the front pushed aside the snow on Main Street, cleared driveways and parking lots. The tourists filed back on the bus, the cheerleaders got back in the van and soon all of the stranded travelers had waved goodbye, eager to get back to their loved ones. Many looked forward to a postponed holiday celebration.

The last to leave were the four Santas, who stayed longer than was necessary in order that they could brighten the holiday celebrations of their hosts. There wasn't a single child in Christmas who didn't get a personal visit from Santa, much to the delight of all.

As the four men finally headed out of town, Sara saw Nikki coming up the street. The young girl hollered and waved, then raced toward the Stable door.

"Hi, Sara! Merry Christmas! I called your house, but your mom said you were over here."

Sara held the door open for her and ushered her inside. "Yup, it's time to finally lock up the place now that everyone's gone."

"Did Mrs. Davis tell you I got to hold the baby?" she asked.

"You did?"

"Uh-huh. Me and Grandma brought breakfast over for them, and Rita let me hold Mary Catherine. She was so cute. Isn't that neat that we had both puppies and a new baby born on the same night?"

"It certainly is," Sara agreed with a smile.

"Do you want to come see Kris's puppies? They're really cute today. They're crawling all over the place.

Grandma had to put them in the laundry room on newspapers because they were messing up everything.''

The thought of going over to the Gibson home and the possibility of running into Joe sent a tremor of excitement through Sara. "Have you had your dinner already?" she asked the child.

"Uh-huh. Grandma says you can come over for cookies and coffee if you want."

"I'd like that. Your grandma makes the best Christmas cookies in town. Just let me lock up the apartment over the bar and I'll be ready."

The sun was sinking fast in the sky by the time Sara and Nikki stepped outside. As they walked back to Alice Gibson's, Nikki kept up a steady stream of chatter, telling Sara what her grandmother had given her for Christmas.

"Even my dad got me something," she told Sara.

"He did?"

"Yup. Remember those bears with the little dresses on them in the craft fair? He wrapped one up for me so I'd have a present from him. Wasn't that sweet?"

"Yes, it was," Sara said candidly.

"My dad went out today."

Sara didn't want to be curious, but she couldn't help asking. "You mean to shovel?"

"Uh-uh. In the car. Grandma told him he was nuts to try to go anywhere and she didn't know what he had to do that was so important anyway."

"What did he have to do?" Sara couldn't resist asking.

"I think he wanted to get some gas for his car."

"He could have gone to the Quick Stop for that."

"That's what Grandma said."

Which only raised Sara's curiosity. What had made

Joe brave the treacherous roads? "Are you leaving tomorrow?"

"I hope not. I have to make sure Kris's babies are okay. Did I tell you what I named them?" Seeing Sara shake her head no she said, "Dasher, Dancer, Prancer, Vixen, Comet, Cupid, Donner and Blitzen. What do you think?"

"I like it," Sara said with a grin.

"If there had been one more we could have named it Rudolph." She ran ahead and tumbled into snow. "You are so lucky to live here. You get to play in this snow whenever you want."

Seeing Nikki frolicking, her arms and legs flailing about like a grounded turtle, reminded Sara of how much fun it had been to be a child. Back in the days when snow wasn't an inconvenience but an exciting adventure.

"There's not always this much snow. Sometimes it's just plain old cold in the winter," Sara told Nikki as she scrambled to her feet.

"Can you eat snow?" she asked, holding a handful up in the air for inspection.

"Only if it's fresh...and I do mean really fresh," Sara answered.

Nikki let the snow fall to the ground. "Did I tell you Grandma bought me a my own pair of ice skates for Christmas? Now I don't have to borrow anyone's."

"That's cool."

"Dad says I might as well leave them here since we don't have any ice arenas close to where we live."

As they neared the house, Sara noticed Joe was outside examining the wiper blade on his sport-utility vehicle. He looked so serious, frowning as he eyed the rubber strip.

On an impulse Sara bent to pick up a fist of snow. She rounded it into a ball and tossed it at him. It hit him on the arm, causing him to glance up in surprise.

"What the...?" he said, looking around until he finally saw Sara.

She smiled and waved at him. "Hi, Joe."

Nikki decided to copy Sara. She, too, scooped up some snow and tossed a ball of it at her father. Her snowball hit him on the leg.

"So you want to play, do you?" he hollered out to the two of them. Then without wasting a moment he crouched, made a couple of snowballs and fired them. Sara managed to evade his bullet, but Nikki couldn't turn fast enough and was struck in the back.

"You're gonna have to do better than that, Joe," Sara shouted back at him, slipping behind a tree, where she formed another snowball in her hands.

Nikki scurried behind the garage so that they could attack him from two sides. What followed was a flurry of snowball activity, amid laughter and shouts of triumph as snowballs either hit their targets or missed. Joe ducked and turned, working frantically to fire in both directions, using the Explorer as his armor.

Suddenly, from behind the vehicle, he called out, "Truce! No more! You got me. I give up."

Sara and Nikki crept out of hiding and walked toward the Explorer, smiles of triumph on their faces. They hadn't taken but a couple of steps when snowballs zinged through the air toward them.

"No fair!" Nikki screamed out, and quickly bent to gather more snow and fire back.

"Keep it up, Nikki. There's two of us and only one of him," Sara called out to her as they bombarded him with the snowballs.

He raised his arms, trying to shield himself from the attack. Closer and closer they crept to him until he fell to the ground moaning, covering his face with his hands. "Ouch! You hit me in the eye."

Nikki's face drained of color. She dropped the snowball in her hand and rushed to her father's side, as did Sara.

"Are you okay?" Sara said at the same time Nikki called out, "Oh no, Dad!"

They both bent over him only to have him reach up with a loud "Aha!" and push them in tandem into the snow. "Gotcha!" he cried out triumphantly as he held them down.

Sara looked at Nikki's startled face and knew once more they had been had. Suddenly, all three burst into laughter.

"It's cold. Let me up," Sara finally pleaded.

Joe removed his hands, and Sara gingerly sat forward.

"I've got snow down my neck," she complained, wrinkling her nose.

"Me, too," Nikki moaned.

"Hey! How about coming inside for something hot to drink?" Alice's voice had all three of them glancing toward the house.

Joe helped each of them up, but it was Sara's hand he held the longest. She didn't want to let it go, but wanted to continue the childlike play. It had been a long time since she had acted so completely without inhibition, and she found it to be exhilarating.

Into the house they trooped, three tired warriors, covered with snow and ice. Alice helped them arrange their jackets to dry on the backs of chairs set in front of the fireplace. Sara noticed that Joe's cheeks were red from the cold, his hair mussed, falling across his forehead in an almost rakish manner. Besides looking handsome, he looked happy and Sara wished that she could capture this moment on film to look back on in the days ahead.

"It's been a long time since my front yard's been a battle zone," Alice commented as the three sat down at the kitchen table.

"Dad doesn't play fair," Nikki complained.

"Men seldom do." Alice chuckled sarcastically.

"That's the way true snowball fights go, don't they, Sara?" Joe looked to her for confirmation.

"When you're fighting boys they do," Sara agreed, and Nikki giggled.

"How 'bout some hot chocolate?" Alice asked the three of them, and got unanimous approval.

"Dad, we don't have to leave tomorrow, do we?" Nikki asked her father as they gathered around the kitchen table. "I mean, we already missed Christmas and I don't have to go back to school until January sixth."

"That's a long time for me to be away from the office."

"I thought you were doing your work from here on your laptop." Alice set a plate of cookies in the middle of the table.

"Some of it I can do here, but I have appointments and meetings to attend. When I left I had only planned to be gone less than a week," he reminded everyone. "It's been two."

"You seldom take any time off. I would think they could get along without you for a few more days." Alice set a mug in front of each of them.

"I want to use my new ice skates Grandma bought me and I want to go sliding with Sara," Nikki said.

Joe looked at Sara. "Sliding? You?"

"Sure. Why not?"

He shrugged and grinned. "I don't know. I just can't picture you on a sled."

"You don't need a sled to go sliding, Joe," Sara reminded him. "Cardboard will do. Don't you remember snow daze our senior year? We all went sliding over at the big bump? Most of us cut up boxes and used that."

"What's the big bump?" Nikki asked.

"It's a hill a little ways out of town where all the kids go sledding," Joe explained. "They call it the big bump because there's this huge mogul in the middle of it that causes everyone to go flying through the air."

Nikki's eyes widened. "Cool! Can we go there?"

"You'll get a sore butt," Joe warned.

"That's what makes it fun," Sara chided him.

"Will you take me?" Nikki looked anxiously at Sara.

"I'm willing to give it a try if your father is," she answered, issuing a challenge to Joe.

All eyes were on Joe, waiting for his answer. "All right. We'll go to the big bump."

"When?" Nikki demanded eagerly.

"Tomorrow?" Joe looked at Sara for confirmation.

"Tomorrow will work for me." She saw him smile then. A slow, wonderful smile that made her insides jitterbug.

"Oh, good. That must mean we don't have to go home tomorrow," Nikki said, clapping her hands together.

"I think you ought to at least stay through New Year's," Alice piped up. "Enjoy Christmas while you can. It won't be long before it's gone."

"But your house won't be gone, will it, Grandma?" Nikki wanted to know.

It was Sara who explained. ''No, everything will still be here. The church, the Quick Stop and all the houses. But your grandmother's right. We won't legally be a town anymore.''

Joe sighed. ''Becoming a part of Denville might actually work in your favor.''

His comment brought daggered looks from his mother. Even Sara scowled at him. ''The people will never change.''

It was Nikki who broke the tension. ''If we stay until New Year's, I'm going to collect a whole bunch of cans and raise the money myself to save the town.''

Joe ruffled her curls. ''You're a good kid, Nik. And yes, we'll stay through New Year's.''

She jumped out of her chair and threw her arms around his neck. ''Thanks, Dad. We're going to have so much fun this week.'' Then she quickly changed the subject and asked Sara, ''I got a Monopoly game. Do you want to play?''

''Sure. I love Monopoly.''

''So does Dad,'' Nikki told her. ''But he's no fun to play with because he always wins.''

''That's because he can't stand to lose money—not even play money,'' Alice added.

''Don't pay any attention to them, Sara,'' Joe instructed her. He rolled up his shirtsleeves and rubbed his hands together. ''Okay, show me the money.''

The four of them played the game and as Nikki predicted, Joe won. Not that Sara minded. It had been a long time since she had played any board games, and she discovered that being with Joe, Nikki and Alice was more fun than she had had in a long time.

When they had finished, Joe insisted on walking Sara home. She didn't protest.

Unlike the days before Christmas when he had seemed tense and uncomfortable being home, tonight he appeared to be relaxed and enjoying his time with his family. Sara wondered what had happened to the power broker, the man who with the utterance of a single word could affect millions of dollars changing hands.

"It was fun being a kid again, wasn't it?" he told her as they stood outside her front door.

"It was. I don't think I've laughed like that since I was a kid," Sara mused aloud.

"I'm glad you came over because I have something for you." He reached into his pocket and pulled out two Nut Goodie candy bars. "It's not much, but considering nothing was open but a few service stations, it's the best I could do."

She took the candy from him and her heart swelled. After all these years he had remembered that Nut Goodies were her favorite. "Thank you. This is so sweet," she said, her voice choking with emotion.

Then he placed a light kiss on her mouth and said, "I like being a kid with you, Sara. I hope you'll come play with me and Nikki this week." And with a wave he was gone.

SARA DID GO with Nikki and Joe often the following week. She felt a bit guilty about having so much fun when everyone else in town was worried about the disincorporation. But Nikki insisted on doing as many winter activities as she could possibly squeeze in. Sara wanted to say no, that she couldn't make it, but the truth was that she enjoyed being with them.

They went sledding, skating and even tried ice fishing. Not once had Joe mentioned kissing her or had he tried to kiss her again, causing Sara to wonder if he wasn't regretting what had happened at the cabin and at the Stable. He had said they needed to finish what they had started, but since Christmas Eve he had made no attempt to do just that.

Then one morning it wasn't Nikki who called but Joe.

December 27, 10:30 a.m.

"I WANT TO TAKE YOU dancing on New Year's Eve."

Joe's words nearly took Sara's breath away. "Where?"

"The Edgewater Hotel in Alex. They're going to have big-band music, noisemakers, party hats...the whole bit. I thought we could do dinner first."

When she didn't respond right away he asked, "Or do you already have plans for New Year's Eve?"

"No, no plans," she answered.

"Then you'll go with me?"

"Yes. I like to dance."

She could hear the smile in his voice. "I know you do."

"What time?"

"Party starts at nine. I thought we'd have dinner at seven....I should probably pick you up around six-thirty."

"Sounds good," she said, trying to calm her racing heart.

"Since it is New Year's Eve and we'll be drinking..." He paused before saying, "Maybe it would be wise to stay overnight at the hotel. That way we wouldn't have to drive home on icy roads late at night."

Again her breath caught in her throat. "We could," she said, licking her lips.

"It would make things easier."

And we wouldn't have to worry about anyone inter-rupting us in the middle of making love, either. She didn't vocalize what she was thinking. She simply said, "Yes, it would."

"I'll call and see what's available," he told her.

"All right. You can let me know."

"Will do. And, Sara, I'm looking forward to beginning the New Year with you," he said huskily.

"Me, too," she said quietly, when she really wanted to gleefully cry out, "Whoopee! I've got a date!" It was a good thing she didn't, for as she hung up the phone she realized that her mother was in the kitchen, a toddler on her hip.

"Was that Joe?" she asked innocently.

"Mmm-hmm," Sara said, getting herself a cup of coffee. "I'm having dinner with him on New Year's Eve."

"I thought so."

"And what made you think so?" Sara asked, curious to know just how much her mother knew of their relationship.

"Just a hunch I had." With the ease of a pro, she moved between the cupboard and the stove, preparing breakfast for her charge.

"Well, as long as it was a hunch and not Alice putting ideas into your head."

Her mother clicked her tongue. "Alice is a sweet woman, and there's nothing wrong with mothers talking about their children."

Sara's cup paused in midair between her saucer and her mouth. "You don't talk about me, do you, Ma?" she asked even though she already knew the answer.

"Of course not."

"But Alice talks about Joe?" she couldn't resist asking.

"Occasionally."

"And?" Her mother tried to change the subject, but Sara wouldn't let her. "Ma, tell me what Alice says about him."

"She says he hasn't been himself lately, thanks to you."

"Why is that my fault?" she asked indignantly.

"Love does funny things to people," she said, strapping the toddler into a high chair.

"Love? Mother, please tell me everyone in town doesn't have us paired up for life," she groaned.

"There's nothing wrong with the two of you being interested in each other."

"We've been having some good times...for old times' sake," She shoved the hair back from her face in frustration. "Just because Midge saw him comforting me the day of the storm and Frank Feester saw us huddled together in front of the fire to stay warm, doesn't mean we're having a romance."

"You forgot to mention your father caught you necking on the front step," her mother said as she spooned creamed cereal into the toddler's mouth.

Sara couldn't prevent the blush that spread to the roots of her hair. "Now I remember the bad part about living in a small town. People talk."

"It's nothing to get upset about. Joe's a nice young man, and I think it's perfectly natural that the two of you want to..." She let the sentence dangle before adding, "Reminisce."

"Does everyone in town think we're involved?" Before her mother could answer, she held up a hand and said, "No, don't answer that. You don't need to." She picked up her cup as she got to her feet.

"Where are you going, dear?"

"Upstairs to get dressed. I'm going ice skating. With Nikki, not Joe," she told her mother as she left the room.

"Whatever you say, dear," was all her mother said.

Sara recognized that tone. It was the one that told her her mother knew differently so there was no point in discussing it. While Sara showered, she thought about New Year's Eve. If she went to Alex and stayed in a hotel with Joe, everyone in Christmas would know about it. There was no keeping secrets about such things in a town the size of Christmas. Not that it mattered to Sara. What did matter, however, was Nikki. She could easily hear the gossip, and that was something Sara didn't want to happen.

That's why when she got out of the shower the first thing she did was to call Joe and say, "Listen, I've been thinking and I don't think it's a good idea to stay at the hotel in Alex."

JOE HALF EXPECTED Sara to call him back and tell him that she didn't want to go out at all on New Year's Eve. He didn't understand why she had sounded so abrupt on the phone when she had nixed the idea of staying overnight at the hotel. When he had asked her for the date, she had sounded as excited about the prospect of spending the night together as he had.

Now she was acting as if it were something she was doing out of duty. Had he misread her interest in him?

"Dad, you're not listening to me."

He looked at his daughter, who stood before him, her hands on her hips. "I'm sorry, Nik. What did you say?"

"Is it true you're going out on a date with Sara?"

"How did you hear about that?"

"Grandma told me."

That had Joe on his feet and moving to the kitchen. "How did you know I had plans for New Year's Eve?"

His mother had a rather sheepish look on her face. "I saw the note next to the phone."

She pointed to a slip of paper that had the phone number to the Edgewater Hotel and the words "Make reservations" written above it. On the same piece of paper he had doodled Sara's name. He scrunched the paper up into a ball and stuck it in his pocket.

"I'm taking her to dinner in Alex."

"Oh."

He knew *oh* meant something more than *oh*. "What?" He pierced her with an inquisitive gaze.

"It's a shame you have to drive all the way to Alex for a party," Alice noted.

"Since the only bar in town is closed and there is no place to eat unless we want to grab a hot dog at the Quick Stop, we really don't have a lot of alternatives, do we?" he drawled sarcastically.

"You could go to the New Year's Eve party at the church."

Joe shoved his hands to his waist. "You've been telling me all week what a terrible day New Year's is going to be because of the disincorporation. Now you tell me the town's having a party."

"Of course they are. We're a strong community. We have a spirit that will not be broken. We just can't sit at home and wait for the boom to be lowered."

"So you're having a party at the church?"

When he made a face, she added, "You don't need to turn up your nose. It's going to be great, complete with a DJ, party hats and noisemakers, plus beer and setups.''

''Somehow the idea of drinking in the church basement doesn't seem right.''

''Well, no one gets drunk, if that's what you're thinking. It's a family party, but that doesn't mean you can't toast the New Year with a drink or two. If you went, you could take Nikki along.''

''I've never been to a New Year's Eve party,'' Nikki said, entering the conversation. ''Darcy Delaney told me her parents had one last year and everybody was kissing everybody in the room when it was midnight. Is that what really happens at those parties?''

''It depends on the people you're with,'' Joe said evasively.

''It's a good thing you'll be with Sara. I bet she won't want to kiss just any old guy,'' Nikki said practically.

The thought of Sara kissing anyone other than him was rather distasteful to Joe. ''We're having dinner and then doing some dancing. It's not like what you see on TV, Nik.''

''Is Grandma right? If you went to the church party I could come, too?''

''Look, Nik, it's really getting late and I think you should go to bed. How about if we talk about this in the morning?''

She didn't protest, to Joe's relief. She simply kissed each of them good-night. As soon as she had gone up the stairs, Joe said, ''Why did you do that? Tell her she could come with me and Sara on New Year's Eve?''

''There's nothing wrong with all three of you celebrating the holiday together. Unless you want to be alone with Sara.'' She fixed him with a penetrating gaze. "Is that what you want? To spend some time alone with Sara?"

She was prying. So this was her way to do it. To find out just what his feelings were for Sara. "What I want is to have dinner at a nice restaurant where there's a menu instead of a buffet table lined with hot dishes."

"Sara's a small-town girl, Joe. You don't need to take her out to some fancy place to make her happy. I bet if you asked her she'd tell you she'd just as soon stay here in Christmas for New Year's."

Joe knew it was useless to argue with his mother. Besides, he knew she could very well be right. Ever since Sara had called to tell him she didn't want to spend the night in Alex, he was having some serious doubts as to what it was she did want.

It didn't help that his mother had to blurt out, "I'm surprised Sara is even going out on a date considering she's off men." •

"Off men?" he repeated. "And what's that supposed to mean?"

"You know she's divorced. Eugenia said she has no interest in dating at all." She quickly added, "Not that it should matter to you. You are, after all, just friends."

"You're right. We're friends," he confirmed, wondering if what his mother said was true or if she was using reverse psychology. Maybe she thought if she told him Sara didn't want anything to do with men, he'd want something to do with her.

Well, he would find out. He would take Sara to Alex. He would wine and dine her, treat her like a queen. This was his chance to charm her, and no way was he going to blow it by going to a church party where every eye in the place would be watching their every move.

No way, no how.

NIKKI GLANCED OUT the window and thought how perfect the nighttime sky looked. There were stars everywhere.

"'Star light, star bright, first star I see tonight. Wish I may, wish I might, have my wish come true tonight.'"

She closed her eyes and said aloud, "Please let Sara be standing next to Dad when the clock strikes midnight on New Year's Eve."

Chapter Eleven

Three days before the big night out, Sara drove to Alex in search of a new dress. A sleek, slinky kind of garment that would knock the socks off Joe. And she found just what she was looking for. It was black with thin little straps, a bodice that hugged her curves and a flared skirt that would swing seductively when they danced to the big-band sounds of the orchestra on New Year's Eve.

While she was in Alex, she treated herself to a manicure, smiling as the short stubby nails were replaced with long, shapely red works of art. Before she returned to Christmas, she stopped at the makeup counter and indulged herself with a new radiant red lipstick and a shower gel that was supposed to have therapeutic powers to help her relax.

For she did need to relax. It had been a long time since she had been out on a date with a man. Right after Paul had left, she had gone through a period when she needed the attention of men to prove to herself that she was still attractive. She had dated friends, friends of friends, and friends of friends of friends. That stage of her life had been short-lived with the discovery that dating hardly made her feel good at all.

So she had stopped thinking about replacing Paul and focused on putting her life back together. Men were not a necessary ingredient to happiness, and it was that conclusion that had brought her to Christmas—along with her financial state. She didn't *want* any men in her life and figured that the last place she would find one would be in her home town of several hundred people.

Now here she was with her heart fluttering every time she thought about Joe. What was it her best friend, Joellen, had said when she had been so disillusioned with the dating scene? "Don't worry about looking for another man. When you least expect it, one will pop up in your life."

Joe certainly had popped into hers unexpectedly. The question was, how long would he stay in it?

It was a question that she had pondered often since he had asked her out. So he wanted to take her out to dinner on New Year's Eve. So he wanted to finish what they had started at the cabin and in the back room of the Stable. So maybe that was all he wanted.

Sex. Maybe he had the hots for her and he figured that while he was in Christmas he might as well make the most of it. Maybe that's why he was taking her to Alex. To not be interrupted the next time he kissed her. Even though she had told him she didn't want to spend the night at the hotel, it didn't mean he hadn't made reservations for a hotel room.

Her mind raced with possibilities, all of them bringing a flush to her face as she contemplated them. What was it about Joe Gibson that made her forget that she didn't want an affair with anyone at this time in her life?

If you're not interested in a relationship with a man, then why are you going out with him? a little voice in her head asked.

She refused to answer that question. There was only one reason why she was going out with Joe. She was falling in love with him.

December 31, 7:30 a.m.

As SARA PADDED into the kitchen, she automatically glanced out the window and gasped. "It's not supposed to snow. Why is it snowing?"

"They say it's another one of those arctic clippers," Eugenia answered, running a sponge over the top of a high-chair tray.

"Another one?" Sara groaned. "How much snow are they predicting?"

"A couple of inches, I think."

"That's what they said at Christmas. It can't snow tonight. We're going to Alex for dinner," she fretted.

"It'll probably let up before this evening." Her mother tried to sound optimistic and reassuring, but Sara wasn't easily comforted.

"And if it doesn't?"

"Plan B?"

This time she groaned even louder. "I am *not* going to the church's New Year's Eve party. Mom, this is not fair. It's the first time in three years I actually have a date for New Year's Eve and it has to do this?" She threw up her hands in frustration.

"You are the Saving Christmas chairperson," her mother reminded her. "It might be nice to put in an appearance...since it is the final hurrah for the town, so to speak."

"I failed, Mom. Do you really think people want to see me on New Year's Eve?"

"You're not a failure, darling," her mother crooned in her maternal voice. Before Sara could argue the point, the doorbell rang, preempting any further discussion as the first of the day-care kids arrived. Sara grabbed a cup of coffee and went back up to her room, where she sat on her bed and willed the snow to stop falling.

It didn't work. By noon the flakes were still coming down. While helping her mother feed lunch to the preschoolers, she kept an eye on the midday news. Her heart sank as the meteorologist indicated a travel advisory for northern Minnesota once again.

"It doesn't sound good, does it?" her mother commented.

"I'm going to be all dressed up and have no place to go," Sara moaned.

"That's not true."

"Oh, Mom, please don't say I can go to the church party."

"Would it be so bad?"

"Yes," she answered bluntly.

Alice didn't say anything for several moments, then she said, "Look on the bright side of things. If you go to the church party, you can bring Nikki along. Alice says Joe seldom does anything without her. It could be it's what he'd prefer, but maybe he thinks he needs to impress you with some fancy dinner in Alex."

What Sara didn't need was for her mother to put doubts in her mind as to Joe's motivations. She already had enough of her own.

It didn't help when Joe called later that afternoon and suggested the same thing.

"It's snowing," Sara said immediately upon hearing his voice.

"I know. The roads aren't in very good shape."

"It's still early," Sara said optimistically.

"It is. I'm willing to make the trip to Alex if you are. But if we go and it doesn't let up, we risk getting stranded there."

"That wouldn't be good," Sara said, hoping he'd contradict her and say he couldn't think of a better excuse to spend the night together. He didn't.

"No, it wouldn't, would it." There was a silence, then he said, "I guess we could always go to the party at the church."

Sara barely managed to stifle her groan. "Sure. Mom says it's a nice party," she managed to get out without choking.

"Yeah, that's what my mom says, too."

He didn't sound any more enthused about than she did. "You could bring Nikki."

"She was already planning to go with my mother…and Sam Hanson."

"Oh."

"We can still make it a special night, Sara."

"Of course we can," she said, trying to mask her disappointment with a false cheerfulness. "My mother's probably right. When the clock strikes midnight and the town ceases to be incorporated, I should be there. United we stand, divided we…" She trailed off.

"All right. That's it, then. I'll pick you up at the same time, I guess, and we'll go to the church dance."

It was only after she had hung up the phone that she added, "And everyone in town will be eyeing us curiously, wondering whether or not we're sleeping together.'' Suddenly, living in a small town didn't have the same appeal it had had on Christmas Day.

The rest of the afternoon she fretted and fussed over the falling snow, praying for a miracle to happen and for the sun to come out and melt everything that had already fallen. It didn't. The snow kept coming down— big, glorious white flakes that any other day Sara would have called beautiful but today were simply ugly.

Shortly after six she slipped on the skimpy black dress, tugging up on the bodice that had looked vampy in the store dressing room but now looked way too low cut. Cleavage wasn't going to cut it at the church party. She dug through her drawers until she found a mohair shawl. She draped it around her shoulders, covering the décolletage that would have been fine in Alex but would be out of place in Christmas.

Not only was the shawl itchy, but it also made her feel like one of the old women she always saw in the back of the church clicking their rosary beads together as they knelt in prayer. Off the shawl came and back into the drawer it went.

Next she sifted through the clothes hanging in her closet. She pulled a short red jacket from a hanger and slipped it on over the dress. In front of the mirror she twisted and turned, tugging on the sleeves, adjusting the shoulders, eyeing the silhouette it gave the dress.

''Not exactly the effect I wanted, but appropriate for a New Year's Eve party at the church,'' she muttered to herself, then went over to the jewelry box to find a pair of earrings to match the ensemble she had created.

When Joe came to pick her up, she was glad she hadn't changed out of the black dress. She could see the appreciation in his eye as his gaze traveled from her head to her toes.

"It isn't easy to be glamorous in a pair of snow boots," she said lightly.

"You look great," he said with a smile that had Sara's heart thumping.

"So do you," she said, giving his formal wear a nod of approval. "Where did you get your tux?"

"In Alex."

She sighed. "I wish we were going there tonight."

"I'm willing to risk the roads if you are," he said temptingly. "I could always walk back to the house and get the car."

Just then her father walked into the room and said, "I don't think that's a good idea, Joe. The roads are bad and it's only going to get worse."

Sara wished a hole in the floor would open and swallow her whole. "He was only teasing, Dad." She waited while her date and her father made small talk. It was so similar to how it had been when she had been a teenager that she felt like a kid again instead of an adult woman who had been married and divorced.

"I'm sorry about that," she said to Joe as soon as they were outside.

"About what?"

"My father giving you the inquisition. And I can't believe he warned you about keeping me safe."

He chuckled. "Now I don't feel so bad. I thought I was the only one being treated like a kid in my mother's house."

Sara glanced back and shuddered. "Oh, good grief. They're looking out the window at us. I can just imagine what it's going to be like at the church party."

"You don't want to go?"

"Not really. Do you?"

"No, I thought you did. At least that's what my mother told me."

"And what mine told me." She giggled. "Geesh, you'd think we were sixteen again."

"Maybe we should act like a couple of teenagers and play hooky."

"You want to skip the church party?"

He held up the brown bag in his hand. "We have the wine. The question is where do we find food?"

"There's nothing open in Christmas…wait a minute. I still have the keys to the Stable. There might be food left in the freezer."

He chuckled. "The way those football players ate? Don't think so."

"Wait here. I'll get the keys." She hurried back up the walk to the house, her high heels dangling from her fingers. Through the hallway, up the stairs, into her room she went, where she found the key ring on her dresser. Along with the keys she grabbed her boom box, then went back downstairs, calling out to her parents, "We've changed our minds about the party. Don't worry about me and don't wait up."

Outside she held the key ring and the boom box up for Joe's inspection. "I thought I'd better bring music. All the records on the jukebox are Christmas carols."

He took the keys and the portable stereo from her fingers. "Wine, music and thou. What more could a guy ask for?" The look he gave her made her hormones sing.

She smiled. "Come with me and you'll see."

They walked the short distance to the Stable, carefully stepping through the accumulating snow. Once inside the bar, Sara removed her boots and slipped on her high heels.

"It's cold in here," she said, rubbing her arms with her hands.

"I'll turn up the heat, you check out the freezer."

To Sara's disappointment, there was nothing in the cooler but a chocolate-cream pie. She carried it out to the bar, where she set it in front of Joe. "Dinner."

He headed for the door. "Stay here. I'll be right back."

Sara watched him dash across the street to the Quick Stop. It wasn't long before he returned carrying a frozen pizza.

"I was just in time," he told her, stomping the snow from his shoes. "They were about to close."

"Mmm—chicken supreme," she said as he handed her the pizza.

"It beats another tuna casserole at the church," he added.

"I'll put it in the oven. You get us something to drink."

While the pizza baked, she slipped into the rest room to freshen up and to remove the red jacket. When she went back into the bar, Joe's eyes darkened appreciatively.

"That is some dress," he said huskily, handing her one of two flutes he had filled with sparkling wine.

"Thank you. Now that we're not in church I figured I didn't need the jacket," she told him, holding his gaze. "You brought champagne?"

"It's a night to celebrate." He lifted his glass for a toast. "To new beginnings, Sara."

"To new beginnings," she echoed.

They each took a sip, then sat down side by side on the bar stools. He had plugged in the boom box, and the sounds of jazz music played in the background.

"I can't believe you found a station that plays jazz," she commented, appreciating the sultry sounds of Kenny G's saxophone.

"I didn't. It's a CD." He held up the plastic case. "Mom said that there was going to be a DJ at the dance tonight so I figured that I would bring it along so we wouldn't get stuck doing the polka all night," he said with a wry grin.

It was the first of many smiles he bestowed on Sara that night as they drank champagne, ate pizza and slow danced to the music on the radio. It was a magical night for Sara, one she didn't want to see end.

As the clock's hands neared midnight, it wasn't just the town's disincorporation she feared, but Joe's departure. After tonight he would go back to California, and she had no idea when she would ever see him again.

At ten minutes to midnight he lifted her chin. "You're looking awfully sad."

She glanced at the clock. "In ten minutes I'm afraid I'll feel like Cinderella at the ball. My handsome prince will disappear, and my home will turn into a pumpkin."

He kissed her, then said, "You need to believe in miracles, Sara."

She looked again at the clock. There were nine minutes to go. "I'm afraid we used them all up on Christmas Eve."

He kissed her again as they continued to dance cheek to cheek. Sara should have been happy, but she couldn't keep from looking at the clock. "Eight minutes to go."

"The town's not going to disappear, Sara," he breathed in her ear.

She clung to his broad shoulders, wanting to believe him. "Now there's only seven minutes left."

"I told you, it's not going to disappear."

"What makes you so sure?"

"Nikki's been wishing on her stars," he said with a charming grin that made her insides flip-flop.

She looked again at the clock. Before she could say "six," he placed his finger across her lips.

"You trust me, don't you, Sara?"

"Yes, but...."

Again he kissed her. And kissed her again. "I need to keep you busy so you quit watching that old clock."

Sara decided he was right. She shouldn't watch the minutes ticking away. But it was Joe who called her attention back to the time. "Look, Sara, it's almost midnight."

They both watched the second hand on the clock as the final ten seconds of the year disappeared. Joe counted them down, then on midnight said,

"Happy New Year, Sara."

"Happy New Year, Joe."

It didn't matter that they didn't have any noisemakers, for the kiss they shared was as explosive as any fireworks that may have lit the sky. This time there were no interruptions when their fingers sought the warmth of skin hidden beneath fabric that was easily pushed aside.

His hands moved slowly, triggering a desire in her she hadn't experienced in a long time. As he patiently caressed her, she realized that no man had ever made her feel this way.

"I've never been able to forget what you do to me," he said when he lifted his mouth from hers.

"And what is that?" she asked breathlessly.

"Feel." He took her hand and placed it over his hardness. "I want you so badly, Sara, I feel as if I could die if I don't make love with you."

"I want you, too, Joe," she admitted, capturing his mouth once more with a kiss that told him she was ready to surrender to the powerful emotions between them.

"We're not seventeen, Sara. This time I'm not sure I'll be able to stop," he warned.

"I don't want to stop." The words came out on a passionate whisper. "Let's go upstairs."

She led him by the hand up the narrow stairs to the sparsely furnished second-floor apartment. With arms entwined they moved into the bedroom, where they danced without music, their bodies rhythmically moving to the beat of passion. Kisses that seemed to have no ending left them breathless and craving for more intimacy.

"Did I tell you this is the sexiest dress I've ever seen?" he asked as he toyed with the thin straps.

"I'm glad you like it." She shivered at the sensations his fingers created. "Did I tell you there's nothing sexier than a man in a tux?" she countered, slipping her fingers inside the pearlized snaps on his shirt.

He planted kisses on her skin as he slid the dainty straps from her shoulders. With a quick zip the dress fell to the floor, and his eyes darkened with desire.

"You like?" she asked as he stood speechless, gazing at her scantily clad figure.

"I like," he murmured, then showed her just exactly how much he did like the way she looked in her bra and bikini briefs, kissing her hungrily while his hands teasingly traced the outline of the skimpy garments. His fingers made a tantalizing journey across satin, exploring every surface hidden beneath the intimate apparel.

Soft moans of pleasure greeted his wandering hands.

As his fingers moved over the satin covering her bottom, she had to stop him. "You're driving me wild."

"That's what I'm supposed to do," he murmured against her mouth, continuing his seductive exploration. He continued to caress and excite her, stopping only when she tugged the shirtsleeves away from his body and needed his arms to rid him of the starched cotton.

As soon as it lay on the floor next to her dress, his mouth found hers and his hands continued to drive her crazy, moving in and out of her underwear, touching and then not touching, creating a longing in her that was so great she could think of nothing but getting as close to him as possible.

She pressed her hands against his bare chest, loving the solid feel of hot flesh. Her fingers began their own journey, across his bare shoulders, down his back and around his waist. He shuddered when they slipped inside his pants, and every moan of pleasure that escaped his throat became a caress in itself.

When he slipped his fingers inside the leg of her briefs, all thinking ceased. She was one with the sensations racking her body as he caressed the moistness of her womanhood and took her to the height of ecstacy.

So intense was the pleasure, her legs weakened and Joe scooped her into his arms and carried her to the bed. They stripped away the remaining clothes and climbed between the sheets of the bed that only a week ago had seen the birth of a new life.

For Sara tonight was another birth—of her love for Joe, a love that had been seeded ten years ago but had lain dormant. Just as had happened ten years ago, their bodies moved together as if they had been made for each other. Only this time instead of stopping Joe from entering her, she welcomed him, her hips lifting in a sensuous invitation.

"I've waited so long for this," he cried out in exhilaration as they made love with an intensity that overwhelmed Sara.

Never in her wildest imaginations had she expected to be so utterly consumed by a man. But she was and as he thrust them both into a spiraling climax, she knew that not only were their bodies united, but their souls were, as well.

When their hunger for each other had finally been satisfied, they lay side by side, both too overwhelmed to speak. Sara could feel Joe's heartbeat, racing as fast as her own.

Finally he placed a butterfly kiss on her mouth and said, "That was incredible."

She smiled lazily. "It was, wasn't it?"

He propped himself up on one elbow. "No amount of fantasizing could have prepared me for this," he said, gently tracing his finger across her breast.

"Have you fantasized about me?"

"Only about a million times," he said, then gave her another kiss, this one longer and more sensuous.

"Thank goodness Chester left this bed," she said on a sigh of satisfaction.

He moved his finger from her breast to her mouth, where he outlined her swollen lips. "And to think I didn't want to stay for Christmas," he mused.

"I never expected when I came home that I'd be having such a romantic New Year's Eve. I am *so* glad we didn't go to the party at the church."

"You mean you like this better than the polka?"

This, Sara discovered, was the touch of fingers on her inner thighs.

"Oh, that's definitely better than doing the polka," she said, her breath becoming ragged as his fingers worked their way upward.

"You're so soft and warm," he said next to her ear, planting tiny kisses along her neck. "I wish tonight never had to end."

His words were like a dose of reality to Sara, who pushed herself up, propping her back against a pillow. "But it does have to end and we need to talk about what happens next, Joe."

He, too, propped himself against a pillow so that they were side by side with their legs stretched out in front of them. He reached for her hands and held them in his.

"I don't want to leave for California and never see you again—which is what happened the last time we spent a night together," he told her.

"I don't want that, either."

"Good. Then we won't let it happen." He paused and she could see he was trying to find the words to say. When he did speak, she was stunned to hear him say, "I love you, Sara. I have since I was seventeen."

Her heart nearly burst with joy. "Oh, Joe, I'm in love with you, too," she said, wrapping her arms around him and holding him tightly to her.

"Then we can work out the problem of two thousand miles separating us," he said with a smile of relief.

She nodded eagerly.

"You told me Christmas was only a temporary stop for you."

"It is, but..."

"Do you plan to return to your work in the theater?"

"No."

He was surprised at how quickly the answer came. "What would you rather do?"

"Have my own clothing store."

"You want to design clothes?"

"Not the stuff for mass production. Just individual creations. I'd like a small shop where women could come and buy clothing that was right for them. Not just the fashions the clothing world wants us to wear."

"So why don't you do it?"

"Oh, I can think of lots of reasons why not. All of them green."

"Money?"

"Bingo. When I told you I'm only here because I had nowhere else to go, I wasn't joking. Not only was my ex-husband a cheat with women, but he was a cheat with money, too. Especially with *my* money."

"You took him to court, I hope."

"Yes. Not that it did much good. As my father says, you can't get blood out of turnip," she said bitterly. "But that part of my life is over. It's all behind me."

"And you have a new beginning. With me," he said, kissing her once more.

She knew she needed to ask the question, as difficult as it was. "And just what are we starting, Joe?"

"A relationship that will last," he answered. "You don't need to worry about money, Sara. I'll take care of you."

Again her heart felt as if it could burst. "That's really sweet of you, but I'm going to get back on my feet again. Ever since I did the costumes for the Victorian Christmas, I've been getting offers to do some tailoring."

"And is that what you want to do?"

"For now. I think it's good that I'm here. I know you never approved of the committee to save Christmas, but coming home and working to help save the town has been good for me.''

"Because you have such a big heart," he said with an affectionate squeeze.

"Because I'm a part of this community, Joe," she corrected him. "We may not have made enough money to have made a difference, but—"

He put a finger to her lips. "You made a difference, Sara. Nikki thinks you're a miracle worker because of the costumes you sew."

Sara grinned. "I know. She's a beautiful child, Joe. You've done a good job with her. It must have been hard when her mother died."

"Yes, it was. She needs a woman in her life. I want you to be that woman, Sara. When we get on that plane tomorrow to go back to California, I want you to be with us."

His request caught her off guard. "Tomorrow?"

"You said there's nothing keeping you here."

She sat staring at him, her mouth agape, anxiety knotted in her stomach. "I'm chairperson for the Saving Christmas committee."

"The deadline has passed."

"But that doesn't mean we've given up. I've been thinking about taking this battle to the state legislature and seeing if we can't get an extension on the deadline and—"

"Sara, it's not your battle."

"Yes, it is, Joe." She stiffened.

"What if I donated the money myself? Then would you come with me?"

"You'd donate twenty thousand dollars to get me to come to California with you?" She stared at him in disbelief.

"Yes, although the reason I haven't done it before now is that I know that it's only a temporary stopgap. Next year you'd be faced with the same problems."

She sat upright, pushing herself away from him. "I realize that, Joe, which is why even if you donated the money, I still couldn't leave. We need to find a buyer for the Stable, for one thing, and try to do some economic development."

"We?" He lifted one eyebrow. "Sara, it sounds as if you feel as if you belong here."

"I do."

"But you haven't lived here in almost ten years," he pointed out.

"Yes, and most of those years I was miserable." She leaned closer to him, her body language begging for him to understand. "Joe, something happened to me this Christmas."

He reached for her hands. "Yeah. Me, too. I fell in love." He gave her his most endearing grin.

"So did I." She squeezed his hand reassuringly. "But that isn't the only discovery I made. I know the Victorian Christmas celebration was a flop, but I learned something really important that day. I realized that I like it here and this is where I belong."

He frowned and pulled his hands back. "What are you saying? That we don't have a future? That these past few weeks have been nothing but a holiday affair for you?"

"No, you know they weren't," she denied passionately. "But you yourself said that you changed your mind about the town. Seeing the caring and trust they share…this town has something you don't find just anywhere."

"That doesn't mean I'd want to live here," he declared irritably.

Her face fell.

He chuckled uneasily. "Sara, you weren't thinking that we would live in Christmas, were you?"

"Nikki loves it here, Joe," she said quietly.

"She hasn't spent an entire winter here." He couldn't keep the sarcasm from his voice.

"It's a good place to raise a family. There's no crime, no gangs...people sleep with their doors unlocked. The people are good people...."

He interrupted her by raising his hands. "Sara, my job is in L.A."

"You told me you can do most of it over the Internet, that as long as you have a PC and a phone, you have an office."

"That doesn't mean I want to work out of Minnesota." He couldn't believe what he was hearing. Did she really think he could so easily pick up and move?

She sounded a bit stubborn as she said, "Well, it's nothing we have to decide tonight, is it?"

"I think maybe it is," he said soberly. "Sara, I love you and I want you to be my wife."

"You want to get married?" The shock on her face told him she hadn't expected he would mention marriage.

"Yes, eventually. Now, I know everything happened rather fast, but I feel as if I've been waiting for you for ten years. I don't want to wait much longer." He pulled her back into his arms and held her lovingly. "Have you ever been to Manhattan Beach?"

"No."

"Then all I'm asking is that you come visit."

"I've been to L.A. I've traveled all over the country

and the more I see the more I realize that this is where I want to be.''

''Just come visit,'' he pleaded.

''I don't have any money, Joe. I told you that,'' she said, her eyes downcast.

''I'll pay for your ticket.''

She shook her head. ''Uh-uh. I can't let you do that.''

''Why not?''

''Because I can't. You don't understand. Paul took nearly everything I had—including my self-esteem. Do you know how hard I've worked just to cling to that? I'm going to get back on my feet financially, but I'm going to do it on my own.''

''Sara, there's nothing wrong with me helping you.''

''Yes, there is. I have to do this myself, Joe.''

''And you insist on doing it in Christmas.''

''Yes.''

He withdrew from her, sliding his feet over the edge of the bed. ''It's late. I should at least make it *look* like I slept in the bed at my mother's. For Nikki's sake.''

Sara nodded in understanding. ''For Nikki.''

As he pulled on his clothes, she asked, ''Joe, you do understand about this money thing, don't you?''

''No, Sara, I don't.'' His voice was flat, not at all like the one that had professed his love for her only minutes ago.

''I'm sorry,'' she said, then turned her attention to her own clothing.

Nothing else was said on the subject. As Joe walked her back home, they were silent.

When they reached her doorstep, he gave her a long, passionate kiss that had her aching to be back in his bed. It told her *she* was the only woman in his life, *she* was the woman he loved.

"I think this has been the best New Year's Eve of my life," he told her, his breath warm against her face.

"I don't want things to be over between us, Joe."

"Me, neither," he told her. "I'll call you later."

She nodded and watched him walk away, wishing she could feel as if there were no reason not to believe their relationship would continue. But she remembered what had happened ten years ago when they had professed their love for one another.

As she got ready for bed she made a New Year's resolution. *I will not let Joe disappear from my life.* But somehow she had a fear that was exactly what was going to happen.

As Joe walked back to his mother's, he couldn't believe what was happening. He hadn't wanted to come to Christmas in the first place, yet now he didn't want to leave. If he had thought he was in love with Sara as a teenager, it was nothing compared to what he felt for her now. Never would he have imagined that spending a couple of weeks with her would give him such a clear picture of what he wanted out of life.

He wanted Sara—to be his wife, to be Nikki's mother. And this time when he married, it would be for all the right reasons.

At nineteen he had been headstrong and impulsive. He had also been trying to forget Sara, which was why he had jumped right into a relationship with Angela. It hadn't mattered that he didn't love her the way he had loved Sara. Because she became pregnant and no longer was it what Joe wanted, but what was best for the baby.

Now he was once more forced to think about Nikki. He knew that she adored Sara, and it angered him that she could put their happiness second to the town of

Christmas. He didn't understand why she'd throw back his offer of money in his face. Didn't she realize he'd do anything for her?

As he climbed the steps to his mother's house, he remembered another time he had come home in the wee hours of the morning. Only that day he had been confident that Sara was his girl and that their future was together. Now he was certain of her love for him, but whether they had a future was questionable.

And once again it was the same thing coming between them: Christmas.

Chapter Twelve

Joe tiptoed into Nikki's room and gently nudged her. Before he had left last night, he had promised her that no matter what time it was when he returned, he'd come in and wish her a happy new year.

As she rubbed the sleepiness from her eyes he said, "Happy New Year, Nik."

"Happy New Year, Dad. Did you and Sara have fun? How come you weren't at the dance?"

"We went to another place," was all he said.

"Did you ask her to come back to California with us? You said you were going to."

"I asked her, Nik, but she can't come. At least not yet."

"But she will come, right?" she asked anxiously.

"I hope so. Maybe in the spring she'll come see us."

"Yeah, after the snow melts. She wouldn't want to leave as long as there's snow." Nikki glanced out the window. "I don't blame her. It's so pretty here and L.A. is so—so dull."

"It's also warm and sunny. And where you live."

She pulled the covers up close to her chin and

yawned. "I guess if I couldn't get you to move up near Lindsey and Shawna's, you're not going to want to move here, either."

"I don't think that's a decision you make on the basis of one visit, Nik."

"Then we'll have to come back a whole bunch of times, right?"

"I don't see that happening," he said candidly. "My work is in California."

"But Sara's here."

He could see that she had jumped to the conclusion he was trying to prevent her from reaching. "I like Sara—a lot. And I know you do, too."

"Yeah. She's really nice. And she's pretty and smart and everything a mom should be."

The statement caught him off guard, although he knew it shouldn't have. As much time as Sara had spent with them the past couple of weeks, it would have been impossible for Nikki not to have grown attached to her. Only he didn't want his daughter to get her hopes up that Sara was going to be her stepmom when he himself wasn't sure that was ever going to happen.

"Nikki, just because Sara and I went out a few times doesn't mean we're necessarily going to get married," he said carefully.

Her face fell. "But you were kissing. I saw you."

"Yes, we were. But love isn't that simple."

She pulled the covers over her head. "It's just like Grandma said. You're too stubborn to see what's right if front of you. Go away. I don't want to talk to you anymore."

"Nikki, you're not being fair," he said gently, trying to pull the covers away from her face.

She held them tightly. "I don't see why you can't

marry Sara and stay here in Christmas forever. I like it here. People are nice to me here. I like living in a fishbowl.''

Alice sat up in bed demanding, ''What is going on?''

Joe rubbed a hand across the back of his neck. ''She's upset about having to leave tomorrow.''

''Of course she is. She needs her grandma.'' Alice climbed out of bed and padded over to her granddaughter's side.

''Well, she doesn't need me. I can't see what's right in front of me,'' he muttered irritably.

His mother said over her shoulder, ''You're right about that.''

''Remind her that it's warm and sunshiny in California and that she has her cousins waiting to have a Christmas celebration with her,'' he shouted after her. ''And people like *me* there.''

January 3, 7:00 p.m.

''FEEL LIKE TALKING ABOUT IT?''

''Talking about what, Mom?'' Sara sat at her sewing machine, altering a dress for Louise Sargeant.

Her mother sat down on her bed. ''I thought maybe you wanted to talk about what went wrong between you and Joe.''

Sara kept working, not wanting her mother to be able to see what was in her eyes. ''What makes you think something went wrong?''

''You mean besides the fact that you've lost your appetite and you haven't mentioned his name once since New Year's Eve?''

''I haven't lost my appetite. It's just that I've been too busy to eat. And you know what they say. Out of sight, out of mind," she answered, still avoiding her mother's inquisitive gaze.

"Not absence makes the heart grow fonder?"

She finally lifted her eyes to look at her mother. "Why should it? He came for a visit, we had some good times. He left. End of story." She returned her attention to the garment in front of her. "So you can satisfy everyone's curiosity by telling them that nothing's going on."

"I'm sorry. I didn't mean to pry," she said apologetically, and got up to leave.

Sara could see that she had offended her mother and immediately felt remorseful. "No, Mom, I'm the one who should be sorry. I didn't mean to snap at you. It's just that I know everyone in town is wondering why we never showed up at the New Year's Eve dance and I don't like the idea of my love life being discussed over coffee."

Eugenia returned and placed an arm around her daughter's shoulder. "No one's talking, Sara."

She made a sound of disbelief. "In a town this size, everyone's talking. Maybe I should have gone to California with Joe."

"He asked you?"

She nodded miserably. "Joe doesn't understand why I can't do that."

"Do you want to move to California?"

"No." The answer came quickly. "This past month has been so good for me. I've realized how much I've missed being a part of this community." She sighed. "When I met Paul I had to choose between being with him and staying here. I chose him and look what happened."

"That wouldn't necessarily happen with Joe," her mother tried to comfort her.

"Maybe not, but I've already had to leave this town for a man once. I don't want to do it again."

"So what's going to happen? Will you carry on a long-distance romance?"

She made a derisive sound. "He doesn't want that."

"And you're worried that this will be the end for the two of you?"

Again she nodded.

Eugenia patted her hand. "I'll tell you what you need to do."

For once Sara wanted her mother to tell her just that. "What's that, Mom?"

"Be patient. If it's meant to be, it'll happen."

Sara nearly groaned. That was it? Her mother's great words of wisdom? It was what she had said hundreds of times when Sara had been a child and every time Sara heard it she wanted to scream. *If it's meant to be, it'll be.*

"There. Now does it help that we talked?" Eugenia asked, giving Sara a gentle hug.

The look on her mother's face was so endearing Sara couldn't say no. "Yes. Thanks, Mom. You're the best."

"Thanks, dear, so are you. Now I'd better let you get back to work."

Only one day had passed since Joe had taken Nikki and gone back to California. One long day in which she had done everything in her power to stay busy, including accepting alterations that she knew wouldn't pay much, but did provide her with income.

She had seen Alice at the Quick Stop this morning and overheard Mabel Jenkins asking about Joe.

"Is he thinking of moving back here?" the older woman had asked Joe's mother.

"Oh, I doubt that. He likes that warm California sunshine," Alice had replied.

It had been a reminder to Sara that any hope she had that Joe would give up the life he had made for himself on the West Coast to move to a town like Christmas didn't have much chance of ever coming true. Ten years had passed, yet nothing had changed. Joe still wanted to stay as far away from Christmas as possible and she wanted to be at its center. How would their love survive?

"DAD, WHAT ARE those people's names? You know, the ones who live across the street in that house with the yellow fence?" Nikki asked her father one afternoon as she sat with her chin on her hands, her face pressed up against the window, watching it rain.

"I don't know. I haven't met them."

"I never see them. They have such dark windows on their car I can't even see who's inside when it drives by."

"They like their privacy."

"You know how when Grandma fell, Hildy next door called the ambulance?"

Joe nodded. "Yeah. What about it?"

"Well, who would help us if we needed someone to call an ambulance for us?"

"You could always go next door to get Mr. Wilson," Joe told her.

"But he's grouchy."

"He wouldn't be if you needed help. He's a nice man."

"But if he wasn't there, where would I go? Nobody talks to anybody in our neighborhood."

Joe hadn't thought much about it until now. "Everyone's busy, Nik."

"Too busy to be nice?" She heaved a long sigh. "And I wish there were kids in our neighborhood."

"You have lots of friends at school. You can invite them over to play."

"It's not the same thing."

Joe had a pretty good idea where the conversation was heading. He expected the next words out of Nikki's mouth to be something regarding how wonderful it was in Christmas. He soon discovered he wasn't mistaken.

"If I lived in Christmas, I would know everyone in my school. The kids in Christmas all go to school in Vargas."

Joe decided to squash the talk about Minnesota. "Hey. I have an idea. How about if we go out for pizza tonight?"

She lifted one brow. "Pepperoni with mushrooms and extra cheese?"

"And a pitcher of root beer."

It was a good diversionary tactic. If there was one thing Joe knew about his daughter, it was the way to her heart. It was with pizza.

However, even pizza only lasted so long. On their way home as the windshield wipers swiped at the rain, she said, "Rain's no fun. I wish we were back in Minnesota. At least there you get to play outside when it rains 'cause it turns to snow."

"Did I tell you Uncle Charlie asked if you wanted to go spend the weekend with Lindsey and Shawna?"

"I can't this weekend."

"Why not?"

"Because Chelsea's having a pajama party on Saturday."

"That's great. You like Chelsea." Joe was relieved to hear Nikki say she was going to spend some time with her friends. The sooner she got back into a routine, the better it would be.

For the rest of the way home Nikki didn't mention Christmas again. Joe knew, however, that life hadn't returned to normal for either of them.

While he was in the office the following day, he discovered that a respectable market analyst in the firm had resigned.

"Can you believe Bill Walters just up and resigned?" one of his co-workers said to him.

"Did he get a better offer from another firm?" Joe asked.

"I wish he had. *That* I could understand."

"You're saying he just quit without any job prospects?"

"You got it." He used a manila folder as a pointer. "Dropped out of the rat race. Decided he didn't want the stress and hassle of working in corporate America. I heard he bought a hobby farm in Idaho. A hobby farm! Can you believe it? He's leaving a six-figure job to raise goats." The guy shook his head in bewilderment.

"Must be a woman involved," Joe automatically said.

"Uh-uh. The guy's divorced, but he does have a couple of kids." As the phone lines lit up he asked Joe, "Who's crazy? Us or him?"

At one time Joe wouldn't have hesitated with his answer. He turned his attention back to his work, but throughout the day he thought about Bill Walters. When an office memo arrived with the information that there would be a going-away party for Bill, Joe wrote the details on his calendar. Maybe by talking to Bill he would find the answers to the questions bothering him.

But Joe didn't need to go to any party to find the answer he was looking for. That night as he sat outside on the patio, he noticed the stars were visible in the sky. He stuck his head inside the house and called out to Nikki.

"Hey, Nik. Come quick. You can actually see stars tonight."

He returned to his chair on the patio and waited, but his daughter didn't come. After calling her a second time and still getting no response, he went upstairs to her room.

To his relief she was there, sitting on the floor, listening to her CD player. Seeing her father, she shoved the earphones aside.

"You must not have heard me calling you. I wanted you to come out on the patio with me. The stars are out."

"I'm listening to Hanson," she said, then slipped the earphones back in place.

He sat down beside her and gently removed the earphones. "What's wrong?"

"Nothing's wrong."

"Yes, it is. You can't fool your dad. When you don't want to wish on a star, there's something wrong."

"Only little kids wish on stars. I'm almost ten."

"Does that mean you've quit talking to your mother, too?"

She looked startled to hear him say that. "You know I talk to Mom?"

"I've heard you."

She looked down at the earphone in her hands. "I suppose you think it's silly, too."

"No, why would I?"

She shrugged.

"I talk to her sometimes, too, Nik," he confessed.

That brought her eyes up. "You do?"

He nodded. "Maybe not as often as you do, but I do talk to her occasionally."

"What about?"

"Mostly about you."

"I talk to her about you," she said with a shy smile. "Mrs. Bergstrom says Mom's an angel now and that we all need angels to watch over us."

"That's true."

"Then you don't think it's dumb that I wish on a star and talk to her?"

"No. Why should I?"

"Remember that pajama party I went to last weekend?" Joe nodded and she continued. "There were a couple of girls there who were older than us and they laughed at me when I made my wish."

Joe gave her a hug. "Aw, Nik, I'm sorry. That wasn't very nice of them."

"That wasn't the worst of it. Chelsea told them I thought the stars were windows to heaven and they all made fun of me. Even Chelsea."

His hurt for his daughter pounded in his chest, as if someone were hammering away with a sledge.

"And she was supposed to be my best friend." Her voice broke and she started to cry. "Now I don't have a best friend. I don't have any friends except Shawna and Lindsey...and they're little."

Joe rocked her in his arms, wishing he knew what he could say to ease her pain. He wished Sara were here.

She had been a nine-year-old girl once. She would have known what to say to Nikki.

Just then his beeper paged him. He looked at the number and knew it was about work. "Hang on, Nik. I have to take this call."

If it wasn't bad enough that he didn't know what to say to his daughter, now he had to leave her alone while he answered some hysterical investor's call.

Later that evening when Nikki was in bed, Joe went back outside. A mist had rolled in off the ocean, masking the stars. He looked across the fence to his neighbor's and saw faces that, although familiar, were still strange to him. Tomorrow he'd get in his car, spend hours in traffic to get into the city, then spend hours listening to panicky investors whine about how much money they had lost, then get back in the car to sit in more traffic so that he could come home and sit alone in his house.

Was this the life he wanted for his daughter? He looked around him and for the first time in ten years wasn't sure.

"SARA, WE HAVE NEWS that's gonna knock your socks off," Alice Gibson told her when she arrived at the council meeting. "We've got a buyer for the Stable!"

"That's wonderful!" Sara cried, hanging her jacket on the coatrack. "Who is it?"

"We don't have that information yet, but Chester's lawyers have told Ed Callahan that it's a done deal," Alice said with a grin that was as wide as the brim on Jean Carson's hat.

Everyone in the room clapped at the announcement.

"And that's not all," Jean added. "As of today, we have received enough money to pay off the bank loan—

thanks to the generosity of our stranded Christmas Eve travelers.''

"That's incredible," Sara said.

"What it is is a miracle," another voice piped up.

"Then the bank granted us the extension on the loan payment?''

"They certainly did. When they heard about the donations we had received, they were downright accommodating.''

"The biggest donation came from the Japanese tourists," Jean told the group assembled in the town hall. "But everyone sent something.''

"Yes, even the cheerleaders made a donation," Alice added. "Just listen to this letter.'' She cleared her throat and read aloud,

"As soon as we got back home, we organized a neighborhood garage sale. This $645.63 is the proceeds we earned. We want you to have it because we think the world will be a sadder place if it loses a town like Christmas.

> Signed,
> the cheerleaders from Monroe High.''

Ed Callahan clomped his gavel on the table and called the meeting to order. The treasurer gave her report, then Jean stood and read aloud the individual thank-you notes they had received. Sara had to wipe a tear from her eye, so moved was she by the messages in them.

"So you see, Sara, they were so impressed with what we take for granted—the warmth and hospitality of our town—they wanted to do what they could to keep Christmas from disappearing off the map.''

"I don't know what to say," Sara said, her voice still choked with emotion.

"We know what we want to say, Sara." Ed Callahan stepped forward with a beautifully wrapped gift in his hand. "It's true we all worked together on this project, but we couldn't have done it without you. And this is a token of our appreciation." He handed her the package.

By now Sara was speechless. She just stood there, choked with emotion.

"Open it!" several people urged her.

She carefully removed the wrapping paper and opened the box to discover a beautiful snow globe inside. In it was a winter scene that could have been Christmas. There was a park with a fir tree decorated with Christmas ornaments and people with songbooks in their hands.

"It's a music box," Alice said softly next to her ear.

Sara wound it up and listened. It played "The Twelve Days of Christmas."

"Thank you. It's perfect," she said, swallowing back the lump of emotion in her throat. "But all of you made this happen. Someone said to me that even if we did lose our incorporation that we had something no one could take away from us. And that's a generosity of spirit and a true concern for one another."

"That's the way it's supposed to be," someone in the audience pointed out.

Several voices echoed the sentiment with "Hear, hear."

"Well, I for one am very proud to call Christmas home," Sara proclaimed. "I've lived in a lot of different places, and there's no place I'd rather be than here."

Applause punctuated her words.

"Does that mean you're going to stay?" Jean asked.

"I hope to. Of course, I have to find a job. A real job," she quickly added with a grin.

"Maybe the new owner of the Stable will let you run it for him. You do a pretty good job of that," Alice pointed out with a wink.

In his usual fashion the mayor took control and said, "I guess this means there's no need for a Saving Christmas committee, is there?"

"Nope. I move we adjourn and exist no more," someone called out.

"Second."

"All in favor."

"Aye," came the collective sound.

"Any nays?" Before Sara could protest, Ed Callahan banged the gavel. "Passed. The committee ceases to exist. On to the next order of business."

And that's that, Sara thought with a smile.

Throughout the remainder of the evening, her thoughts weren't on the business at hand, but on what Alice had told her. Although she had acted happy to hear the news, she had hoped that Chester would rent her the apartment over the bar. Although she appreciated her parents' generosity, she knew that she couldn't go on living with them indefinitely. If her alterations business continued to grow, it wouldn't be long before she would be able to afford her own place.

As soon as the meeting was over, Sara approached Alice in hope of finding out more about the new owner. "Haven't you heard anything about this new guy?"

"No, only that he supposedly wants to find someone to manage the place."

"How did he hear about it? Chester hasn't even listed it with a real-estate agent yet."

"Apparently he was here on Christmas Eve."

"He was one of the stranded travelers?" That had Sara's mind racing with possibilities. "It couldn't be the lady wrestlers or the cheerleaders or the football players," she told Alice.

"And I doubt Rita Davis is going to give up her dental practice to move here," Alice added.

"It could be one of the Santas...."

"They were looking for booze...all four of them."

"What about the nuns?"

"Buying a bar? Uh-uh."

"The carolers were pleasant...."

"But connected to some church."

"Then it must be one of the Japanese tourists. They were awfully taken with the legend of Paul Bunyan."

"My money's on one of the Santas," Alice wagered. "But we'll soon find out. Ed says the new owner's coming the first of February."

"That soon?"

"Guess he's ready to become a part of this wonderful town," Alice said with a grin.

"I wish I knew what his plans were for the apartment upstairs. I had hoped Chester would rent it out to me."

"There's only one way to find out. Ask," Alice stated simply.

"You're right. I will. On February first I will be there to find out for myself."

And she was. However, the minute she stepped onto Main Street, she saw that it was unlikely the new owner would let her rent the upstairs. A moving van sat out front. The bar didn't need any more furniture, which meant it had to carry stuff for the apartment upstairs.

Sara would have turned around and gone home, but her mother had made a batch of banana-nut bread for the new members of the community and it was in her hands waiting to be delivered. So she marched up to the door and knocked.

No one answered, so she tried the doorknob. It was unlocked. She stepped inside, calling out, "Anybody here?"

Not a sound could be heard.

The bar looked the same as it had on New Year's Eve. Empty. The chairs turned upside down on the tables, blinds closed, lights off.

She walked past the bar into the kitchen, where she set the bread on the counter. "Hello?" Still she found no one. Not in the storage room. Not in the walk-in cooler. Not in the women's rest room. She didn't check the men's. She was about to knock on the door leading to the apartment upstairs when the sounds of tubas filled the air.

It startled Sara into a gasp. What were tubas doing in the Stable? Then she recognized the song they were playing. It was "Crazy," the same song she and Joe had danced to over and over on prom night.

Sara's heart began to thump as if she were watching a suspenseful movie and waiting for the killer to jump out of the dark passage. Gingerly she crept toward the swinging doors, her mouth growing dry. Slowly she pushed one of the panels aside.

As she suspected, Joe was leaning up against the bar, arms folded across his flannel shirt, a smile on his face. Behind him were the ten tuba players who had played at the tree trimming in the park. Sara could only stare in disbelief as they finished their song.

When they had finished, she looked at Joe. "Are you...?" She couldn't get the rest of the words out.

"The new owner? Yes."

She covered her mouth with her fist to try to stop the tears, but it was useless. They poured down her face, and she quickly backed into the kitchen. Joe came charging through the swinging doors.

"I hope those are tears of joy and not tears of horror," he said.

For an answer she threw her arms around him and hugged him. "Of course I'm happy. I just can't believe you gave up your job and moved here for me."

"I didn't."

She backed away from him. "You're not moving here?"

"Yes, I'm moving here, but I didn't give up my job. I just became my own boss." He fished a business card out of his pocket and handed it to her.

"You're going to work here?"

"As long as the phone lines don't go dead," he quipped. "And working for myself, I can have as many or as few clients as I want. After all, I want to be able to have time to run the bar."

"You're gonna run the bar?"

"On a part-time basis," he said with a grin. "Actually I was hoping to find someone who could take care of the day-to-day running of the place. Someone who has lots of patience, who is great with people...someone who knows how to take care of others."

Sara shook her head, grinning. "So that's why your mother asked me if I wanted to run the place."

"Do you?"

"It depends. Is this a paying position?"

"Oh, definitely."

"With time off?"

"Yup."

"And benefits?"

"Great benefits. It comes with a completely furnished apartment upstairs. And your own personal assistant."

"An assistant?"

"Yes." He walked over to the apartment door and whistled through his teeth. Down the steps came Nikki, an apron wrapped around her middle, a broom in her hand.

"Hi, Sara. I'm back!" she said with a huge grin.

Sara opened her arms, and Nikki dropped the broom and ran into them. It was another tearful, joyful reunion. When they had exhausted the hugs and tears, Joe asked, "Does this mean you accept the position?"

"Only if it comes with a lifetime guarantee," Sara asked.

"Then it's a deal," Joe said with a smile. And from the bar they heard the tubas play the bridal march.

Epilogue

" 'Star light, star bright, first star I see tonight, wish I may, wish I might, have my wish come true tonight.' "

Nikki sat on the bench in her grandmother's backyard. It was the first day of summer—her first day of summer in Christmas. And the stars were very bright.

"Thanks, Mom, for making it happen. The wedding was perfect. I just want you to know that even though I have a new mom, I'm never going to forget you. Please keep the window open, okay? And thanks for being my angel."

Look for CORPORATE COWBOY,
Pamela Bauer's next book from
Harlequin American Romance,
available in February 2000.

Starting December 1999, a brand-new series about fatherhood from

HARLEQUIN®

AMERICAN ◆ ROMANCE®

*Coming in January 2000—
a very special 2-in-1 story...*

Two sexy heroes, two determined heroines, two full romances...one complete novel!

Sophie's a stay-at-home mom.
Carla's a no-nonsense businesswoman.
Neither suspects that trading places for a week
will change their lives forever....

HIS, HERS AND THEIRS (#808)
by Debbi Rawlins
January 2000

*Join us for twice the fun, twice the romance
when two sisters-in-law trade places and fall in
love with men they wouldn't otherwise have met!
Only from Harlequin American Romance®!*

Available at your favorite retail outlet.

HARLEQUIN®
Makes any time special ™